This spring break

is going to change

our lives . . .

While Gabrielle and Megan bantered back and forth, Alyssa sat silently and thought about what had just happened at Dune Buggies. She was practically engaged to Brock Jorgensen, and yet she had thrown herself into the arms of another boy. And not just another boy, but a perfect stranger. And then she had let him kiss her. But the very worst part of the whole thing was that she had enjoyed it. Maybe Megan was right. Maybe this spring break would change her life forever!

**Don't miss these exciting books
from HarperPaperbacks!**

FRESHMAN DORM
by Linda A. Cooney

#1 *Freshman Dorm*
#2 *Freshman Lies*
#3 *Freshman Guys*
#4 *Freshman Nights*
#5 *Freshman Dreams*
#6 *Freshman Games*
#7 *Freshman Loves*
#8 *Freshman Secrets*
#9 *Freshman Schemes*

HORROR HIGH
by Nicholas Adams

#1 *Mr. Popularity*
#2 *Resolved: You're Dead*
#3 *Heartbreaker*
#4 *New Kid on the Block*
#5 *Hard Rock*
#6 *Sudden Death*
#7 *Pep Rally*

Books in the **SPRING BREAK** series:
#1 *Road Trip*
#2 *Beach Boys*
#3 *Last Fling*

ROAD TRIP

Alison Page

HarperPaperbacks
A Division of HarperCollins*Publishers*

Special edition printing: July 1994

HarperPaperbacks *A Division of* HarperCollins*Publishers*
10 East 53rd Street, New York, N.Y. 10022

Produced by Daniel Weiss Associates, Inc.
33 West 17th Street, New York, New York 10011.

First printing: March, 1991

Printed in the United States of America

HarperPaperbacks and colophon are trademarks of
HarperCollins*Publishers*

10 9 8 7 6 5 4 3 2

ROAD TRIP

On Tuesday afternoon, the mall in Leesville, Georgia, was jammed with high school students picking up last-minute necessities for the spring break, which was scheduled to begin at exactly one minute after three on Friday afternoon. More than half the senior class of Leesville High planned to spend the ten-day vacation in Coconut Beach, Florida. It would be the last great social event of the school year, and nobody wanted to miss it.

In the midst of the crowds streaming up and down the broad concourse, a strikingly beautiful girl stood in front of the window of Johnston Jewelers. Alyssa Chandler clutched several bulky shopping bags in each hand as she looked thoughtfully at the gold wedding rings behind the plate glass. A week ago, her boyfriend Brock had pointed to the engagement ring with the

1

largest diamond and declared, "That's the ring for you."

"I don't know, it seems so . . . so big," Alyssa had replied. "Maybe something simpler."

"No way," he'd insisted. "I want the world to know you're going to be my wife."

And that had been that. Brock Jorgensen was very possessive and very proud. The license plate on his Jeep CJ8 Scrambler read, "BJS CJ." For Christmas their freshman year, he had given Alyssa a silver ID bracelet with "Brock" engraved on it in big, fancy letters. And in their junior year, Brock had given her a promise ring, another sign that he considered Alyssa his, exclusively and forever. Alyssa Chandler and Brock Jorgensen had been going steady for so long that just about everyone referred to them as "Brock-n-Alyssa," as if they were one person. And now that it was known they would be attending the University of Georgia in the fall, just about everyone assumed they would be getting married shortly after graduation.

Alyssa stepped back and stared at her dim reflection in the jeweler's window. She looked intently into her own dark, green eyes, and tried to detect a change in them. No, she decided. She didn't look any different, in spite of the fact that things were changing inside her in the most bewildering way.

"Hey, Alyssa!" Jenny Marcus called from the door of the video arcade.

"Hi, Jen," Alyssa said as the other girl joined her.

"Why are you studying the wedding rings?" Suddenly Jenny smiled as if a pleasant truth had just dawned on her. "Have you and Brock finally set a date?"

"No, we haven't set a date," Alyssa said patiently. "I'm just meeting Brock here."

Jenny took a sip of the extra-large soda she held in her hand. "Well, when you *do* set a date, will you tell me right away?"

"Of course." Alyssa swallowed her annoyance and smiled. How could Jenny know that lately any mention of marriage to Brock made her nervous?

"Your wedding will be the event of the century," Jenny continued. "Leesville's star halfback weds the homecoming queen."

"Well, I don't know about that," Alyssa said. She could feel a blush rising to her cheeks.

Just then the girls were distracted by the approach of a tall, lanky boy with sparkling blue eyes and a crooked smile. "Aren't you coming to Orange Julius?" Tom Hooper asked.

Tom was referring to the gathering at a fast-food joint that Shannon Dobbler, Leesville High's head cheerleader, had called earlier that day. As the most popular girl in the senior class, Shannon thought it her duty to organize the class's plans for the ten days at Coconut Beach.

Alyssa frowned. "I forgot all about it. When is everyone meeting?"

"Any minute," Tom said as he checked his watch. "I'd better scoot. I promised our fearless leader I'd take notes." Tom grinned and loped off toward Orange Julius.

"To be honest," Alyssa said, "I don't really see why we need a meeting. What's there to plan? Everybody has a ride and a place to stay."

"True. But you know how bossy Shannon is! She has to leave her mark on everything." Jenny slurped up the last of her soda.

Alyssa shrugged and laughed lightly. "I know. Anyway, it might be fun to get everyone together before we leave Friday afternoon."

A burst of laughter sounded from nearby where a crowd of seniors had already gathered.

"You're right! C'mon!" Jenny reached for Alyssa's elbow.

"I can't. I have to wait for Brock, remember?"

"Oh, right. Well, I'll see you in school then. 'Bye!" Jenny hurried off to join the group.

A moment later, a pair of arms circled Alyssa's waist and a familiar, deep voice rumbled in her ear. "Three guesses, and the first two don't count."

4

Alyssa smiled and automatically leaned her head against Brock Jorgenson's broad chest. "You're late," Alyssa sighed. "As usual."

"And, as usual, I have a good excuse." Brock rested his chin on top of Alyssa's head. "I was on the phone with my grandparents. They can't wait to see us."

Brock and Alyssa had been invited to stay with Brock's grandparents in their cozy frame house in Coconut Beach, right on the Gulf of Mexico.

Brock released Alyssa and pointed to a shiny gold-and-diamond wedding set. "Have you decided on our rings? Mr. Johnston said he'd put a hold on whatever we choose, but only for seven days."

"We don't have to make any decisions now," Alyssa said. "Let's talk about it later, okay?"

"Aw, come on," Brock said. He pulled her close to him and nuzzled her long, thick, auburn hair. "Why don't you just try on a few rings?"

Alyssa shook her head. "We don't have time. Besides, you promised to help me pick out a present for your grandparents."

Brock pointed to the shopping bags Alyssa was carrying. "I thought you'd already bought them something."

"No, silly, these things are for me." Alyssa laughed. "I needed a few things for the beach."

"A *few* things?" Brock repeated, as he took the bags from her. They began to stroll down the wide aisle of the mall. "It looks as if you bought out the store."

"Well, I'd only intended to get a pair of shorts and some suntan lotion, but I got a little carried away."

Brock shook the smallest of the three bags. "So what's in here? A bikini?"

Alyssa swatted him playfully. "You wish."

"*Is* it a bikini?" Brock asked seriously. "I don't think I like the idea of my fiancée wearing a bikini in front of all those slobbering wolves at Coconut Beach."

Alyssa sighed. It was so typical of Brock not to want her to wear anything too revealing. "It's not a bikini. If it makes you feel any better, I'll be wearing my jade green tank suit."

"The one with the back cut down to there?" Brock ran a finger down her spine; goose bumps scurried up Alyssa's arm.

"Yes." Alyssa giggled. "That one."

Brock grinned. "Okay, you can wear it. But only at my grandparents' house."

"Don't worry." Alyssa smiled sweetly. "I promise to wear a trench coat when we go to the beach."

Brock put down the shopping bags and pulled her close to him. "Come here, green eyes."

6

Alyssa buried her face in Brock's chest. She was confused by the conflicting thoughts that suddenly began to tumble around in her head. One minute she felt claustrophobic about their relationship, and just wanted to run away. The next minute she felt all warm and happy inside, and couldn't imagine how she had ever doubted her love for him.

"You know I'm crazy about you," Brock murmured.

Alyssa lifted her head and met his lips in a kiss. "I know."

While the majority of her friends were discussing vacation plans at Orange Julius, Megan Becker was at home.

Megan Becker was one of five varsity cheerleaders at Leesville High. And though it was a tradition for the seniors, particularly the popular ones like those on the cheerleading squad and the football team, to spend spring break at Coconut Beach, Megan wasn't at all sure she would be going. Her parents were having second thoughts about letting their daughter travel without adult supervision, but Megan hadn't given up hope.

She threw open the door to her bedroom and struck her best fashion model pose. She was wearing a neon pink-and-black bikini from which the price tag still dangled.

"So, can you picture me, lying on the hot, white sands of Coconut Beach, glazed with cocoa butter, gazing into the baby blue eyes of the cutest hunk to ever hit Florida?"

Megan's fourteen-year-old sister, Sara, who was sitting cross-legged on the bed, applauded. "You look fabulous!"

"Really?" Megan stood in front of the full-length mirror hanging on the back of her closet door. "You don't think it's too small?"

"Of course not," Sara assured her. "It makes your waist look teeny-tiny."

Megan piled her wavy, blond hair on top of her head and studied her reflection. Though she desperately wanted to be considered glamorous, the dusting of freckles across the bridge of her turned-up nose labeled her terminally cute.

"I wish I had gotten a tan and lost ten pounds before this trip," Megan complained. She stuck her tongue out at her mirror image. "Shannon Dobbler and Monica Levitts spent all last month at the faker baker."

Sara's face scrunched up quizzically. "What's that?"

"The tanning salon, silly," Megan replied.

"Well, Shannon and Monica can afford it,"

Sara said. "I'd like to hear what Dad would say if you asked him for money to get a tan."

Megan giggled, then lowered her voice, and in her best imitation of her father, growled, "Buy a tan? Since when does anybody *buy* a tan? Lay out in the backyard if you're so fired up to fry your skin." She shook her head and squeezed her eyebrows together like her father always did when he had made a decision. "But *I'm* not paying for any tan."

"That's good," Sara said. "Now let me hear what he's going to say when Mom tells him you want to spend ten days in a motel with three other cheerleaders and no chaperon."

Megan put her hands on her hips. "There'll *be* a chaperon. Shannon's older sister, Tiffany, is going to stay with us."

"Tiffany Dobbler?" Sara giggled. "Get real. She may be in college, but she's only a year older than you guys. If you think she's going to pay the slightest bit of attention to a bunch of high school seniors, you're seriously deranged."

Megan put a finger to her lips. "Sssh. Of course I know Tiffany won't be a *real* chaperon. But I want Dad to think she's very responsible. So don't say anything, okay?"

Sara hung her head. "I won't. I'm not a kid, you know."

"I know. I'm just warning you to be careful." Megan smiled and ruffled her sister's hair.

Megan walked to the door of the bedroom and quietly opened it. She tiptoed into the hall. For the past hour, ever since her father, a pilot, had returned from his latest trip, her parents had been closeted in the den.

"I wish I could hear what they're saying," Megan complained when she returned to her room. "They've been locked up in there forever!"

"I'm sure Dad's doing his, 'But she's too young!' routine."

"Too young?" Megan scoffed. "I've been eighteen for two whole months and I'm about to graduate from high school!"

"Don't lecture *me*," Sara said, as she adjusted her glasses on her nose. "Lecture Dad."

"I don't have the nerve," Megan admitted. She checked her watch. "I just wish they would hurry up. I have to finish packing, and Shannon's invited some of the most popular kids to her house tonight so I can teach them the Limbo."

"The *what*?" Sara asked.

"The Limbo. Haven't you ever heard of it? It's sort of a dance, sort of a game, done to Caribbean music. Two people hold a bamboo pole between them, and another person has to pass under the pole without falling down."

"Sounds really challenging," Sara cracked.

"It is. Because on every turn, the pole gets lower and lower to the ground. Finally, the only way to get under the pole is in a backbend position—without putting your hands on the ground!"

"Why would anybody want to do *that*?"

"Because it's fun.

"And why would Shannon ask *you* to teach everyone?" Sara asked doubtfully.

"Because I told her I was an expert Limbo dancer."

"And are you?"

"Well, I've never actually done it before. But you know I'm pretty flexible. And if I fall, or get stuck in a backbend, I'll just have to be rescued by a gorgeous Florida hunk!"

Megan fell back on her bed with a dreamy sigh. Her headboard bumped against the wall and a pair of maroon gym shorts that had been hanging from a nail fell onto her head. "Oooh, gross," she cried, as she shoved them away.

"Where'd you get those, anyway?" Sara demanded.

"They belong to Randy Tyler," Megan replied. "Shannon dared me to sneak into the boys' locker room one day."

11

"You're kidding!" Sara exclaimed. "And you did?"

Megan nodded proudly. "And I 'borrowed' these while the boys were in the shower."

"I'd never be able to do something like that," Sara said in an awed whisper.

Megan hung the shorts back up beside her other "trophies"—a turkey feather she'd plucked from the headdress of the Ashton High Indians mascot at halftime, a "No Admittance" sign from backstage at the Leesville Auditorium. She had gotten that the night rock star Terry Randall had played there. Underneath the sign hung a black-and-white photograph taken at the senior carnival fundraiser. Megan had volunteered to be the girl in the dunking booth. Tom Hooper was in the foreground of the picture, his arms raised above his head in triumph. Megan glared at the camera from inside the tank.

The phone rang and both girls dove for it.

"I'm sure it's for me," Megan said, as she scooped up the receiver. "Hello?"

"Well?" a voice said impatiently. "What's the word?"

"Oh, hi, Shannon. My parents are still talking it over." Megan leaned back against her headboard.

Shannon sighed dramatically. "I hope you've

told him that *everybody* who's *anybody* will be in Coconut Beach."

"That's not exactly a selling point for parents," Megan answered ruefully. "I did remind them this week would be the last time the seniors would be together before everyone goes off to college. And I told them your sister will be chaperoning us."

"Good. Listen, we're just about to leave the mall, but I wanted to tell you that if it turns out you can't make it, Monica has a friend from Ashton who said she'd take your place. And she needs to know soon."

"How soon?"

"Like within the hour."

Megan groaned. "God, Shannon, my parents only take a few minutes to decide about the trip, and you've already given up my motel reservation?"

"Oh, Meg, don't be so dramatic," Shannon retorted. "It's not that we don't want you to stay with us. We're just trying to keep the costs down. And look, even if your parents say no, I'm counting on you to show up at my house tonight to give everyone Limbo lessons. You promised, you know."

Megan hesitated, but only for a moment. "I know, I know. I'll see you later. 'Bye." She put the phone back on the hook. "Shannon's getting anxious, and so am I," she told Sara.

"Why did you wait until the last minute to ask Dad if you could go?" Sara asked.

"First of all, he's been gone for the past two weeks," Megan said. "And second, if you give Dad too much time to think about anything, he'll always say no."

Sara reached into one of the three open suitcases on the floor, pulled out one of Megan's dresses, and held it up to her. "I really hope Mom and Dad let you go," she said. "That means they'll *have* to let me go when I'm a senior."

Megan grinned at her younger sister. "They'd probably say yes to you anyway. You always get to do things I wasn't allowed to do at your age."

"Right. Name one."

Before Megan could answer, there was a knock on the bedroom door.

"Meg, honey?" her mother called. "May we talk to you a minute?"

Mrs. Becker never called her daughter "honey" unless she had bad news. Megan took a deep breath and opened the door.

A backyard away from the Becker home stood a rambling, white, Victorian house, its eaves and wraparound porch decorated with elaborate wooden gingerbread trim. Gabrielle

Danzer sat by the attic window, watching a bank of clouds lumber across the Georgia sky.

"Okay, sky. Inspire me!" She turned to her cat who lay curled on a cushion under one of the eaves and whispered, "I don't think the sky's listening."

Gabrielle spent most afternoons in the little attic studio, painting the everchanging view from the window. From her perspective, the town of Leesville was a broad canopy of green tree-tops studded here and there by a white church steeple.

"I guess it's up to my own genius." Gabrielle stood before her easel and picked up a paint brush. On the easel sat a canvas already covered in broad strokes of blue and white. Gabrielle stared at it thoughtfully with her large, luminous eyes. Her father told her she'd inherited those eyes from her mother.

Mrs. Danzer had died several years ago. After her death, Gabrielle had transformed the attic into her own special place. Once it had been cluttered with musty old trunks and sagging, overstuffed chairs. Now the sloping walls were hung with bright canvases that reflected the various stages of Gabrielle's interest in painting.

Though Gabrielle loved being surrounded by color, she insisted on dressing only in black— black turtlenecks, black jeans, black mini-skirts, blouses, and boots. Some kids at school called her the Dark Lady of Leesville, but Gabrielle didn't care. The austerity of black made her feel more like a serious artist.

Gabrielle lowered her paintbrush and walked closer to the window. The Becker house had recently been painted a loud, electric blue. "Who would paint their house electric blue?" she wondered. "Who but Megan Becker?"

Gabrielle smiled sadly. She remembered all the time she had spent in that house. She and Megan had been inseparable in elementary school. They'd shared many of the same classes, had been members of the same Brownie troop, and had even worn their hair in the same style.

Gabrielle wasn't really sure when her friendship with Megan had ended. She stood on tiptoe to peek down at the old magnolia tree. She and Megan would meet at its base and talk for hours. Then the tree had seemed very special. Now, it was just one of the many trees that had grown up between their yards.

Suddenly, the Beckers' back door flew open, and Megan ran down the short flight of steps.

"Speak of the devil," Gabrielle said.

She watched Megan trip over a skate, then pick it up and fling it into the trees. Someone must have called from inside the house, because Gabrielle saw Megan turn and gesture angrily.

At the same moment a knock came on the attic door. Gabrielle started.

"Gabby?" her father's voice called. "Are you in there?"

"Yes, Dad," she answered. "I'm painting."

"Who's with you?"

"Nobody." Gabrielle glanced over at the cat and added, "Except Miss Amelia."

Mr. Danzer, a dark-haired man with a shaggy moustache, popped his head into the room. "I know I heard you talking to someone."

Gabrielle rubbed her nose and left a streak of blue paint on her cheek. "Miss Amelia is a wonderful conversationalist."

Mr. Danzer perched on the arm of an antique velvet armchair, one of the few pieces of furniture Gabrielle had not thrown out. "I've got some good news."

Gabrielle set her brush down on the tray of the easel and wiped her hand on a rag. "What is it?"

"I got the fellowship from the Melziner Foundation."

"Oh, Daddy!" Gabrielle ran to her father and wrapped her arms around his neck. "That's wonderful!"

The Melziner Foundation awarded a prestigious annual grant to three composers. The grant allowed each composer to work for sev-

17

eral weeks on one of their own compositions in Washington, D.C., with a famous conductor. Her father, who taught music at Leesville High, had applied for the grant for five years in a row.

"There's just one small hitch," he said.

Gabrielle pulled back from her hug. "What's that?"

"I start immediately. As in tomorrow. One of the winners dropped out and, as first alternate, I was called."

"Tomorrow!" she gasped. "There's barely enough time to pack. And what about getting our plane tickets? We're flying to Washington, aren't we?"

Mr. Danzer took a deep breath. "There's another small hitch. I'm going alone."

Gabrielle's heart sank. She had been looking forward to spending spring break with her father. "But why can't I come, too?"

"I'm sorry, Gabby. I'm not permitted to bring anyone with me. Besides, the housing I've been given is in one of the men's dorms at Georgetown University. And even if I were allowed to bring you, you'd be alone most of the time. I'll be hard at work from morning 'til night."

"I wouldn't care," Gabrielle protested. "Daddy, please, let me come, too. I could stay some place nearby. I know how to entertain myself. Besides, I'd only be able to stay until school starts again."

"I'm sorry, Gabby. It's not possible for you to come with me. But I don't want you spending your vacation here, all alone, either." Mr. Danzer took his daughter's hands in his. "Which is why I called Kate."

"Aunt Kate?" Gabrielle looked perplexed. "What's she got to do with anything?"

"She's invited you to spend the week with her in her new condo."

"In Coconut Beach?" Gabrielle's eyes widened in horror.

"Yes. I thought you'd be pleased," her father continued earnestly. "You spend so much time by yourself and you work so hard in school and on your painting. My trip to Washington provides the perfect opportunity for you to take a *real* vacation."

"Dad!" Gabrielle moaned. "I'd rather die."

Mr. Danzer looked dismayed. "I thought you'd be happy about the news."

"Dad, don't you know? Coconut Beach is one long strip of sleazy motels and night clubs. Hordes of girls lay on the beach all day in skimpy bikinis while hordes of brain-dead jocks drool all over them."

Her father stood up and sighed. "No, I didn't

really know what Coconut Beach was like. Well, that's that, then."

Gabrielle looked at him suspiciously. "What's what, then?"

"I'm not going off to Washington and leaving you here by yourself," he replied. "But I'm also not going to subject you to a miserable vacation. I'll just have to refuse the grant."

Tears of frustration welled up in Gabrielle's eyes. She knew how much the Melziner Fellowship meant to her father. There was no way she would let him turn it down.

"No, Dad," Gabrielle said calmly. "I'll go to Coconut Beach. It won't be so bad. I like Aunt Kate." Gabrielle could hear her voice beginning to break. She kissed her father on the cheek. "Who knows? Maybe I *will* have a good time."

Mr. Danzer smiled fondly at his daughter. "Maybe you'll even find a deserted stretch of beach where you can do some sketching."

Gabrielle swallowed the lump in her throat. "Yeah. Look, Dad, I'm going to go for a drive, get some air. I'll be back soon."

Without waiting for his reply, Gabrielle left the attic and hurried out of the house. When she slid into the driver's seat of the old Mustang that had once been her mother's, her hands were shaking so badly she could barely put the keys in the ignition. Finally she succeeded, and the engine rumbled to life. With a hasty glance over her shoulder, Gabrielle backed out of the driveway and onto the street.

Suddenly, there was a horrible squeal of tires and then a sickening crunch of metal. Gabrielle was jerked forward violently. It took her a moment to realize what had happened. Someone had run into her!

Megan sat frozen behind the wheel of her car and stared out at the crumpled hood in stunned silence. A plume of steam hissed from the radiator. Gingerly she rubbed the bump on her forehead and tried to reconstruct the last few minutes, which, right now, were one confused blur in her mind.

She remembered getting into her car, intent on arriving at Shannon Dobbler's house before everyone else did, to deliver her terrible news in private. She remembered backing out of her driveway, making a right at the first corner, and another at the next, onto the street leading toward the main thoroughfare. And she remembered that as she crested the small hill just about mid-block, a dark shadow had appeared in front of her, and there had been a tremendous jolt and a loud crash.

"I hit someone!" she gasped.

Megan pulled herself out of the little Toyota and almost fell to her knees. Her legs were rubbery and barely able to support her weight. Holding onto the fender with her right hand, she walked around to the front of the car. It was a smashed-in tangle of twisted metal and chrome. She tugged helplessly at the crumpled fender above the left wheel.

"Oh, my God!" Megan groaned. "My parents are going to kill me."

While Megan was examining what was left of the Toyota, the dark-haired girl who had been at the wheel of the Mustang had hurried back to examine her car. She was standing only inches from Megan. "What have you done?" the girl cried. "My rear bumper is completely destroyed!"

Megan recognized the voice. It belonged to Gabrielle Danzer and it was Gabrielle's '68 Mustang that Megan had hit. "I swear I never even saw you!"

"That's because you were driving too fast," Gabrielle answered angrily.

"Too fast!" Gabrielle's accusation was too close to the truth, and Megan snapped back to life. "I was only going twenty. If I had been going any faster, your entire trunk would be missing." She put her hands on her hips. "It's your fault I hit you. Why didn't you look before you backed out into the street?"

"I *did* look," Gabrielle shot back. "But I didn't expect some maniac to come speeding over the hill."

Megan folded her arms stubbornly across her chest. "Any policeman who witnessed this accident would say I had the right of way."

"Accidents are something you'd know about," Gabrielle retorted. "No wonder kids at school call you Becker the Wrecker. You've been in more accidents than anyone I know!"

Megan winced. It was true she had had four accidents in the last nine months. The first had happened in a downpour, and her car had been crammed with friends. She hadn't even seen the other car pull out in front of her. Luckily, no one had been hurt, just scared. Then she had been rear-ended in the school parking lot by Buddy Pearson. Another time she'd leaned over to change the radio station and accidentally side-swiped a parked car. But the worst had been when she totaled her car outside of the TKE fraternity on the Georgia Tech campus. Instead of watching the road, she'd been watching some guys play football. Her parents had grounded her for a month after that one.

Now they'll probably ground me for life, she thought.

"Besides," Gabrielle continued firmly, "it's clear I didn't back into you. You hit me." She pointed to the crunched metal and peeling paint that ran the length of what used to be the Mustang's rear left fender. "It's your fault, and your insurance will have to pay."

Megan knew Gabrielle was right. From the position of the cars, and given her driving record, any judge would rule in Gabrielle's favor.

"What in the world's happened here?" a voice exclaimed. Megan saw Gabrielle's father hurrying down the front steps of the old Victorian house.

"My Mustang was destroyed, that's what happened," Gabrielle said.

"Are you all right?" Mr. Danzer asked both girls.

"I bumped my head on the steering wheel," Megan admitted, gently rubbing her forehead. "But it's nothing serious."

"No double vision or headache?" he asked.

"No." Megan almost wished there were. Then maybe her parents would feel so sorry for her they wouldn't punish her.

"Well, then, let's inspect the damage." Mr. Danzer walked around the two cars. Every now and then he paused, stroked his moustache, and uttered a thoughtful, "Hmmm." Finally, he got down on the ground and ran his hand under

Megan's car. After a moment he stood up and brushed his hands together briskly.

"Well, neither car is damaged beyond repair." He smiled sympathetically at Megan. "It looks worse than it is."

"With my parents, looks are everything," Megan replied glumly.

Mr. Danzer nodded. "Do you want me to talk to them?"

Gabrielle couldn't believe her ears. First, her father had decided to send her off to Aunt Kate's for spring break. Now he was offering to help her ex-best friend. Her world seemed about to collapse around her. As if to prove it, she suddenly found herself thinking a thought worthy of Megan Becker. Her problems were solved! She couldn't possibly drive the crumpled Mustang to Coconut Beach. Now her father would *have* to take her with him to Washington.

"I guess this means I won't be going to stay with Aunt Kate in Coconut Beach. The Mustang will never make it in this condition." Gabrielle tried her best to keep the hopefulness out of her voice.

"You're going to Coconut Beach?" Megan's misery was complete. Even outsiders like Gabrielle Danzer would be there, while she stayed all alone in Leesville. It was too depressing.

"I *was* going." Gabrielle looked at her father, and this time she couldn't keep the excitement out of her voice. "I guess I'll have to go to Washington with you, Dad."

"Now, Gabby," Mr. Danzer said, pleasantly but firmly. "Lots of other kids are driving down to Coconut Beach. Half of my music students, for instance. Surely there must be someone who can give you a ride."

Gabrielle shook her head. "I don't think so. All of my friends are staying in Leesville."

Megan raised an eyebrow at the mention of Gabrielle's friends. As far as she knew, Gabrielle Danzer spent most of her time alone. It wasn't that the kids didn't like her, it was just that she didn't seem to like them very much.

"Megan, you're going to Coconut Beach, aren't you?" Mr. Danzer asked. "Could you give Gabby a ride?"

"In what? Look at my car!" Megan replied. "And besides, I'm not going."

It was Gabrielle's turn to look surprised. She knew that everybody who was anybody at Leesville High was going to Coconut Beach and that Megan Becker, the official Life of the Party, wouldn't miss this blow-out without a good reason. "Why aren't you going?" Gabrielle asked.

Megan poked the front left tire of her car with the toe of her sandal. There was no point in

28

lying. Things were bad enough. "My parents won't let me. They say I have to have a chaperon." Suddenly, the words tumbled out of her mouth in a torrent. "Everyone else's parents are letting them stay at the Flamingo Motel without a chaperon. I think my parents want me to rot in my room until I graduate."

"Chaperon." Mr. Danzer stroked his moustache slowly. "If that's all your parents are worried about Megan, maybe you could stay with Gabrielle at her Aunt Kate's. The two of you would be company for each other."

Neither girl replied. It had been ages since they had spent any time together. They weren't even friends anymore. What was Mr. Danzer thinking?

"The two of you could have a fabulous time. Kate's condo is right on the beach, you know."

Still, neither girl replied. Finally, Gabrielle cleared her throat. "Um, Dad? What about the car situation? Ours are both wrecked. And Aunt Kate's apartment might be really small. What if she doesn't have room for two guests?"

"No problem. Kate told me she has an extra bedroom and a fold-out couch in the living room." He ignored the pleading look in Gabrielle's eyes. "And the Mustang doesn't look beaten, just bruised. I'll get it into the body shop tomorrow morning, and it'll be ready by Friday afternoon."

Gabrielle slumped against the side of her car. Why was her father determined to ruin her life? Her one remaining hope was that Megan would bow out. She couldn't imagine that Megan wanted to spend spring break together any more than she did.

"So, Megan, what do you say?" Mr. Danzer smiled at her encouragingly. "I'd be happy to talk to your parents and give them my sister's credentials. She's head nurse at Centennial Hospital in Coconut Beach. Quite a responsible person."

Megan took a deep breath. She wanted to tell Mr. Danzer that the prospect of ten days with his daughter didn't thrill her in the least. She was desperately trying to think of a polite way to turn down his offer when a car came over the hill and slowed down to get a closer look at the accident.

The car was Shannon Dobbler's. Megan turned away, hoping vainly no one would recognize her, but it was too late. The car had stopped.

"Hey, it looks like Becker the Wrecker's been at it again," Tom Hooper shouted as he pulled himself through the open back window and sat with his hands resting on top of the car.

Shannon Dobbler leaned out of the driver's window and pushed her sunglasses on top of her blond head. "Well, what did your parents decide? Are they letting you go to Coconut Beach?"

"Not after this accident," Tom cracked.

Megan took a deep breath. She didn't like lying in front of Mr. Danzer, but she hoped he'd understand. "Actually, my dad wasn't too keen about my being crammed into a motel with so many kids." Megan glanced at the Danzers and plunged ahead. "But I've come up with a solution to that problem. I'll be staying somewhere else."

"What?" Shannon's sunglasses fell forward onto her nose. "Where?"

"With Gabby's aunt." Megan gestured casually to Gabrielle. "She has a condo right on the beach."

Tom Hooper whistled appreciatively. "Class act, Becker."

Megan smiled. Trust Tom to make her feel better. She ran her hand through her hair and fluffed it nonchalantly. "Once we get settled in, and if it's okay with Gabby's aunt, maybe everybody could come over for a visit."

"A party at a condo?" Tom banged his hands on the top of the car. "All right!"

Megan looked nervously at Gabrielle. She

31

hoped she wouldn't spoil her bluff. Gabrielle silently stared back at her.

"When was all this decided?" Shannon asked suspiciously.

"Well . . ." Megan looked at Mr. Danzer and found some encouragement in his understanding expression. "You see, it was like this. I was out for a drive and Gabby and I sort of, um . . ."

"Ran into each other," Gabrielle finished in a deadpan voice.

"Ran into each other!" Tom hooted with laughter and slapped the top of the car again. "I'll say."

"So we got to talking," Megan continued quickly, "and Gabby told me she was staying with her aunt in Coconut Beach and I told her that you could easily replace me with a girl from Ashton. So," Megan said with a shrug, "I agreed to stay with Gabby on one condition."

"What condition was that?" Shannon demanded.

"That Gabby drives."

A wave of laughter exploded from the back seat. Megan grinned. She felt her life of the party spirit charging back. "Yep, ol' Becker the Wrecker has decided to turn in her keys. At least for the time being."

"Yeah, until your parents give them back to you," Tom cracked.

While Megan and her friends were exchanging barbs, Mr. Danzer whispered in his daughter's ear. "Don't worry, Gabby. I know you'll have a good time. You and Megan will have a chance to get to know each other again. You used to be such good friends. What do you say?"

"What *can* I say, Dad?" Gabrielle gestured in Megan's direction. "But did you hear her? She's already arranged a party at Aunt Kate's." Gabrielle frowned. "You may find both your sister and your daughter at your door in Washington!"

"Hey, Megan," Tom Hooper called, "we missed you at the meeting."

Shannon flipped her hair over her shoulder. "We planned the convoy, the trip to Porter's Island, everything. Look, just because you're not going to be staying with us doesn't mean you can get out of showing us the Limbo tonight. We're counting on you."

Megan tensed. How could she promise to be at Shannon's tonight after what she'd just done to her car? Her parents would need at least an evening to lecture her on safe driving.

"I don't know if I can make it tonight, Shannon. Maybe I can show everyone the Limbo tomorrow at lunch break," Megan suggested.

"Break! The magic word!" Randy bellowed. He and Tom leaped out of the car and ran in circles with their hands held above their heads, whooping all the while like maniacs.

Mr. Danzer laughed good-naturedly at their antics, while Gabrielle covered her eyes with her hand. *This spring break is going to be the most hideous, gruesome experience of my life,* she thought.

3

"All right, campers!" Megan Becker shouted to the line of cars that was growing in the parking lot of Leesville High School on Friday afternoon. "Let's get these Winnebagos in formation!"

Megan wore a pair of white shorts and a flowered halter top. Round-framed sunglasses hung around her neck and a neon-green visor perched on her head. The visor's brim proclaimed "The Party Starts Here." The only thing unusual about Megan's outfit was her footwear—big, blue diving flippers. She flip-flopped along the line of cars, stopping here and there to crack a joke.

Gabrielle had pulled her Mustang up to the end of the line. She watched Megan parade up and down the parking lot. "This must be part of her campaign for Class Clown," she said to no one in particular.

Her father may have strong-armed her into joining the other seniors in Coconut Beach, but even he couldn't persuade Gabrielle Danzer to leave her signature black clothing in Leesville. Gabrielle wore a short black skirt and a sleeveless black shirt. Her silver bracelets jangled when she ran her hand through her hair. "Let's get this show on the road," she said, again to no one in particular.

Tom Hooper emerged from the school building wearing a mask and snorkel. A Donald Duck innertube encircled his waist. Gabrielle found it hard to believe that this was the Leesville High senior class president.

He's just as goony as Megan is, Gabrielle thought.

Tom pretended to swim his way along the line of cars. He breaststroked to Megan, and the two of them fell into an imitation of synchronized swimmers.

When he reached the head of the line, Tom took the snorkel out of his mouth and hopped up on the hood of Brock Jorgensen's Jeep. "I have an announcement to make," he shouted. "There will be a slight delay in the Coconut Beach convoy. Please stay in your cars and wait for further instructions."

Brock Jorgensen hit the horn with the palm of

his hand. "Put a cork in it, Hooper, and get off my car," he yelled good-naturedly.

Alyssa, beside Brock in the front seat, pressed her fingers to her temples and rubbed them in a little circle. Her headache had begun at lunch, when Brock had invited Mike Bibbit and Nat Farrell to ride with them to Coconut Beach. Alyssa had hoped the ride would be a chance for the two of them to be alone together and to talk about their relationship.

Brock slipped on his sunglasses and the neon-green straps looped down across his cheeks. A mini-cooler full of sodas sat on the floor between them and Brock nodded toward it as he reached over and squeezed Alyssa's knee. "Hey, 'Lyssa, pop me a root beer." Brock turned his head toward the back seat. "How about you guys?"

Mike Bibbit stuck out a beefy hand. "I could use a drink. And got any skarfing material?"

"There's a few bags of chips in the straw bag by your feet, Mike," Alyssa said politely.

"Excellent." Mike dove into the bag and retrieved a bag of corn chips and one of the sandwiches Alyssa had packed for Brock. Though they were planning on stopping at Carter's Truck Stop for dinner, Alyssa knew Brock would get hungry again before long.

Alyssa tugged at the pull-tab of a can of root beer. The brown, foamy liquid spurted out and splattered all over her pink-and-white-striped T-shirt and her pale pink shorts.

"Whoa, it's Ol' Faithful!" Mike Bibbit chuckled through a mouthful of chips. Nat Farrell guffawed loudly.

Brock quickly grabbed the can and put his mouth over the top to stop the overflow. Alyssa reached for some paper napkins she had tucked in the side of her purse.

"This is terrible," she moaned. A big brown stain had formed right down the center of her T-shirt, and some of the soda had splattered onto her white leather sandals. "My whole outfit is ruined."

"Hey, 'Lyssa, don't worry about it." Brock gave her knee another squeeze. "It's spring break. People are supposed to get down and dirty."

"Yeah, look at Mike's shirt," Nat answered. "It's already got a big glob of mustard on it. And what's this?" he pointed to a red smear on Mike's shorts.

"That's ketchup," Mike said. "From lunch."

Having Nat Farrell point out the stains on Mike Bibbit, the Human Garbage Disposal's clothing, didn't make Alyssa feel any better. The root beer had seeped through to her skin and she felt sticky. She pressed a napkin against the wet stain.

"I know how to cheer you up," Brock declared. "I was going to wait until we got to Carter's Truck Stop to tell you my surprise. But I think I'll just tell you now."

"Surprise?" Alyssa continued to dab at the brown stain.

"Coach Slater is letting me out of the first week of practice." Ted "Touchdown" Slater was the coach of the football team at the University of Georgia.

"I don't understand. Why?"

"For a honeymoon, of course. That means we can get married even sooner than we'd hoped!"

Alyssa stared blankly at Brock.

"I figured we'd get married on August seventh and start our honeymoon on the eighth." Oblivious to her shock, Brock wrapped his arm around Alyssa's shoulder and pulled her toward him. "Six days in sunny Mexico! Isn't it great? I can't believe our luck."

Alyssa pulled away from her boyfriend's strong embrace. "August seventh? That's barely five months away."

"Now, don't worry about a thing." Brock smiled fondly at Alyssa and patted her knee. "I talked to your mom last night and she said she'd have plenty of time to make the arrangements."

"You talked to my mom and your football coach before you talked to me?" Alyssa leaned back against the passenger door. If Mike Bibbit and Nat Farrell hadn't been in the back seat, she would have screamed, "How could you?" But she was too much of a lady to raise her voice in public.

"Of course. I talked to them first because they're the ones who are running the show." Brock reached for Alyssa's hand again and she gave it automatically. "Let's face it, if the Coach didn't let me out of practice, or your mom and dad refused to give their consent, we'd just have to wait."

"But what about *me*?" Alyssa asked in a quiet, tense voice.

Brock glanced over his shoulder at his friends and then back to Alyssa. "What do you mean, 'What about me?' You're the star of the show!" Brock smiled and Alyssa realized that, once again, he was acting more like a father indulging a fussy child than a boyfriend discussing something important with his girlfriend. But that was Brock's usual way of smoothing things over. Whenever they disagreed, Brock refused to pay attention to her point of view. Instead, he would wrap her in his strong arms and whisper endearments in her ear. For a long time his tactics had made her warm and tingly inside. Lately, they had just made her angry.

"Hey, Bibbit, how does August seventh sound

to you?" Brock asked his friend. "It's the first Saturday in August. Have to clear it with my best man!"

Mike took another big bite of the sandwich Alyssa had made for Brock and mumbled, "Sounds great. I'll be there."

"I don't believe it," Alyssa said, almost to herself. "Now he's asking *Mike* before me."

Brock looked stung. "But I did ask you."

"No, you *told* me," Alyssa corrected him. "That's very different." Though her tone was calm and polite, Alyssa felt as if a cord was wrapped around her throat and being pulled tighter every minute.

"Alyssa, maybe you're not feeling well. You've been a little tense all day." Brock shifted closer to her. "Let me rub your neck. Do you have another of those headaches?"

Alyssa felt dangerously close to screaming. When she spoke again, her voice had lost its steeliness. "I'm fine. Really."

"Alyssa, something *is* the matter with you," Brock insisted. "You almost sound as if you don't want to get married!"

Things Alyssa had been thinking about for the past few months but had never spoken about, were suddenly at the tip of her tongue.

"Maybe I'm just not ready to have you decide everything for me. Maybe I'll never be." Alyssa laughed bitterly. "My God, Brock, you even decided where we'd go for our honeymoon."

"You always said you would like to go to Mexico," he answered smoothly.

"That's beside the point!" Alyssa took a deep breath to calm herself. "All I'm saying is that marriage should be a partnership, one in which two people *talk* to each other."

Mike Bibbit took the opportunity to cut in. "And that's just what you two need to do. Talk. Alone. Now."

Alyssa's cheeks burned with embarrassment. She leaned forward to let Mike and Nat out of the jeep. "You'll have to excuse me. I didn't mean to create a scene. I'm just a little upset right now."

Brock tried to save face with his buddies by joking. "Alyssa has what's known as cold feet. Funny, I always thought only guys got that."

"Yeah, well, listen," Mike said, as he leaned partially through the window. "Nat and I may check out the singles scene down the line. Hitch a ride with a few babes and catch up with you later."

"That's cool." Brock waved easily. "You can join us at Carter's Truck Stop."

Mike and Nat walked off and Alyssa sat quietly, staring ahead at the gravel parking lot. She was vaguely aware of Mike Bibbit talking to

Megan Becker, nodding, then jogging past them.

Before Brock or Alyssa could break the awkward silence, Tom Hooper banged on the hood of the jeep and shouted, "All right, Jorgensen, let's get this junk heap on the road."

Brock slammed the gearshift into first and peeled out of the parking lot, almost running over Tom's foot in the process.

The long line of cars made its way through Leesville, then out onto the highway and through the green Georgia countryside.

Alyssa sat stiffly in her seat. Every now and then she would open her mouth to speak but lose her courage. It had been like this for years. She'd see Brock's jaw muscles twitching, and whatever she'd wanted to say had suddenly seemed not worth the risk of a fight.

After a full forty-five minutes of silence, Brock spoke. "I can't believe you made a total fool of me in front of my friends."

Alyssa blinked in astonishment. She'd anticipated one of several comments, but that was definitely not one of them. Brock's selfish remark gave her courage. "Is that all that matters to you? What your friends think? What about what *I* think?"

"You don't understand. Mike's my best

43

friend," Brock said tightly. "He's going to be my best man. Or, he *was*."

"What's that supposed to mean?" Alyssa asked quietly.

"You called off the wedding, didn't you?"

"I didn't call off anything," Alyssa retorted. "I said that I didn't appreciate your setting a date without consulting me. But to be honest, Brock, I can't say I was completely surprised. You've always made all the decisions for us. Lately, I've realized I don't want to live my life through someone else."

"Well, how *do* you want to live your life?" Brock's tone was unmistakably condescending.

"I'm not exactly sure, yet. But I want to find out. And I just don't know if I can do that and be married to you at the same time. We're so young, Brock. Maybe too young to get married."

"So, you *are* calling off the wedding?" Brock snorted in disgust.

"I . . . I didn't say that!" Alyssa protested.

"You might as well have." Brock pushed the accelerator to the floor. Alyssa watched the speedometer go from sixty to seventy-five.

Alyssa closed her eyes and prayed they'd reach Carter's Truck Stop in one piece. And soon.

Gabrielle parked the Mustang in front of Carter's Truck Stop and sighed with relief. An hour-and-a-half of stupid jokes from Mike Bibbit and Nat Farrell had been almost more than she could stand. And traveling with Megan was no better. She had insisted they stop three times before even leaving Leesville, once at Discount Drugs for suntan lotion, once at Mordy's Drive-In for a soda, and once at Jack's Gas Station to use the restroom.

"Last one in is a rotten egg!" Megan called as she raced past Gabrielle toward the glass door of the café.

"Looks like that'll be you, Farrell." Mike Bibbit shoved Nat with his elbow, and Nat sprawled over a low hedge that bordered the sidewalk around Carter's. With a roar, Nat leaped to his feet and hurled himself across the hedge in full tackle. The two boys rolled around on the grass, enjoying the hoots of encouragement they received from Megan.

Gabrielle hung back in the parking lot and watched Megan and the boys finally pass through the door of the famous old café. From where she stood, she could just make out through the big picture window the boisterous action inside.

"Dinner with the popular crowd," Gabrielle said aloud. She took a deep breath, walked up to the door, and stepped inside.

It was the usual division of cliques—jocks and cheerleaders at a few tables in the corner, student council types at a table across the room, and in the center, two tables of girls, and one table of boys. Gabrielle didn't feel comfortable joining any of the groups, though she was friendly with several of the girls at the center tables.

Just head for the counter and people won't stare at you, she thought.

Ryan Stevens and Tom Hooper were perched on stools at the old-fashioned Formica counter, devouring a huge platter of onion rings. Two seats away, a girl with long, auburn hair sat staring down at a plate of cottage cheese and shredded lettuce.

That looks like Alyssa, Gabrielle thought as

she neared the counter. *Alone. But that's not possible.*

Gabrielle quickly glanced over at the table of jocks. Sure enough, Brock was sitting with his pals. Mike Bibbit pulled up a chair next to him and helped himself to a fistful of french fries from Brock's plate.

Gabrielle looked back at Leesville's resident beauty and slipped quietly onto the worn red leather stool next to her. She gave the waitress her order for a hamburger with tomato, onion, and lettuce, and a side of fries. The waitress hollered over her shoulder in the direction of the kitchen. "Drag another cow through the garden, and hit 'em with spuds!"

Gabrielle couldn't help but laugh and her laugh caught Alyssa's attention. She looked at Gabrielle with red-rimmed eyes. Little smudges of black mascara stained her cheeks.

"Hi," Gabrielle said. When Alyssa didn't answer, Gabrielle continued nervously. "I'm Gabrielle Danzer. We have English Lit and Physics together."

Alyssa shook her head and smiled. "I know. Last year we had History and Geometry together. And the year before that, we were in Mr. Stubbson's homeroom."

Gabrielle was surprised. She always thought of herself as an invisible person at Leesville

High. For a moment, she didn't know what to say. "Um, you have a good memory."

"I also had your dad for Chorus two years in a row." Alyssa pulled a paper napkin from the metal dispenser and dabbed at her eyes. "He's nice."

"Thanks," Gabrielle said. She rested her elbows on the counter. "I think so, too."

A burst of deep laughter sounded from Brock's table. Alyssa looked back down at her cottage cheese. A large tear dropped onto the edge of the lettuce and she blindly reached for the napkin dispenser.

"I'll get it," Gabrielle said, as she handed her another paper napkin.

Alyssa took it and blew her nose. "You'll have to excuse me," she said. "Brock and I had a misunderstanding on the way down, and I can't seem to get a grip on myself."

"I'm sure you guys will work things out," Gabrielle said lamely.

Alyssa shook her head. "I don't think so."

Another burst of laughter sounded from the table of jocks, and Alyssa winced. "Brock appears to be taking our fight pretty well, doesn't he?"

"He does seem to be feeling no pain," Gabrielle said carefully.

"Well, that's fine with me." Alyssa straightened her back. "If he wants to ignore what's happened between us, then I can, too." She picked up her fork and dug into her cottage cheese.

Gabrielle didn't know what to say to Alyssa. She really didn't know her at all. And she had virtually no experience in boyfriend troubles. None of the girls she was friendly with at school had boyfriends, and though Gabrielle had gone on several dates, she had never had a steady boyfriend. Gabrielle looked nervously over her shoulder for Megan. Megan must be used to this sort of thing. The couples in Megan's crowd were always breaking up and switching partners, and Megan was often right in the thick of it, playing the go-between. Gabrielle spotted her standing at the cheerleaders' table.

"Excuse me, Alyssa," Gabrielle said, as she got up from the counter. "I need to talk to Megan for a minute. I'll be right back."

Gabrielle felt silly and even a bit mean running from Alyssa, but having Alyssa confide in her had made her panic. Gabrielle made her way through the crowded café to the far table of cheerleaders.

"Uh, Megan?" she said. "Could I talk to you for a minute?"

Megan checked her watch then looked at

Gabrielle with annoyance. "We've only been here ten minutes. We can't be leaving yet."

"I don't want to leave. I just want to talk to you."

Megan looked down at her friends who were busy eating. Not one of them had made room for her to sit down.

"Go on with Gabrielle, Megan," Shannon Dobbler said as she dipped an onion ring in a blob of ketchup and popped it in her mouth. "She obviously means more to you than the squad."

Megan swallowed. So that was it. "Oh, come on, you guys," she said with a nervous laugh. "I may be rooming with Gabby, but I'll be spending most of my time with you."

"How nice." Shannon dabbed at the corner of her mouth with her napkin. "You know where we'll be. Give us a call sometime." Shannon turned her back on Megan and leaned close to Monica.

Megan tried to catch the eyes of one of the other girls but each continued to stare down at her plate. She turned to Gabrielle and feigned a bright smile.

"Okay. What is it you wanted to talk to me about?"

Before Gabrielle could answer, their attention was caught by a loud movement at the jock's table. Brock had stood up and shoved his chair back. "BJ's CJ is ready to roll," he announced. "Anybody who's riding with me, pay up, and let's go." Brock tossed some change on the table and strode toward the cash register.

All eyes watched as Brock stopped behind Alyssa. She remained in her seat, continuing to stare down at her half-eaten meal. Brock stood behind her for almost a full minute. Neither of them spoke. Finally, he turned and called back to his table. "Bibbit, there's plenty of room for you and Farrell if you want to ride with me."

When Brock continued toward the cash register, Alyssa slid off her stool and, without meeting anyone's eye, walked out the door and straight to Brock's Jeep. She pulled open the door and yanked her bags out of the back seat. Her hands were shaking with anger, and her face was red with humiliation. She couldn't believe Brock had been so callous. He had announced to the entire room that he was leaving without her. He had never done anything like this before.

"I'll show him," she muttered as she tossed her tapestry-print suitcase onto the pavement. "I'm going back to Leesville!" Alyssa tugged at the straw picnic bag that Mike Bibbit had so thoroughly ravished. Somehow it had gotten wedged under the seat. Alyssa put her foot against the side of the jeep and pulled with all her might. Suddenly, she lost her balance and fell backward onto the pavement.

"Careful!" a voice called from behind her.

The jolt of hitting the hard ground, coupled with the awful scene with Brock, made Alyssa's eyes brim with tears. She roughly pushed her hair out of her face and turned to see a stranger kneeling beside her.

"Are you all right?" the boy asked. He had light brown, wavy hair and warm, brown eyes that were filled with concern.

"No, I'm *not* all right," Alyssa replied as she made an attempt to collect the food and Thermos bottle that had rolled out of the straw picnic bag. "But it has nothing to do with falling down and making a fool of myself in front of everyone." Without even looking, Alyssa knew that just about everyone in the café had been watching her through the picture window.

"Don't mind them." The boy picked up an apple that had rolled under Brock's jeep and rubbed it on his shirt. "Here, have something to eat. I find that food always makes me feel better in a personal crisis."

Alyssa looked up at him and he smiled, revealing a tiny dimple in his right cheek. The boy held out the apple to her. Alyssa took the apple and bit into it loudly, at the same time looking defiantly at the picture window of the café.

"Feel better?" he asked, as he gently took her elbow and helped her to her feet.

Alyssa nodded and held up the apple. "A little silly, but better, thank you."

"Do you need help with your bags?" he asked.

Alyssa shook her head. "No. I can carry them myself." The boy handed her the suitcase, and Alyssa looped the picnic bag over her shoulder. "Thank you for all your help," Alyssa said. She took a deep breath and prayed for the courage to go back inside. With a brief nod, she headed for the door.

"It was my pleasure," the boy called after her.

Megan, Gabrielle, and everyone else in the café watched as Alyssa shouldered her way through the door and without a word made her way directly to the ladies' room.

As if on cue, everyone turned to look at Brock, who stood silently at the counter, one hand gripping its ledge. A tense moment passed in which no one dared move. Finally, Brock shook his head, turned, and left the café. No sooner had the glass door swung shut behind him than the café was in an uproar.

Megan whistled softly. "Wow. I never thought I'd see the day Brock and Alyssa would fight."

"That's what I wanted to talk to you about. Didn't you see Alyssa sitting alone before? Aren't you going to help her?"

53

"Why should I be the one to help Alyssa?" Megan asked in surprise.

"Isn't she your friend?"

"I barely know her," Megan replied. "We have a few classes together and we worked on the Let's Go Reading Project last summer. But Alyssa spends all her time with Brock and his family. And I spend all my time with the cheerleaders." Megan frowned. "At least, I used to."

"Well, we can't just leave her alone in there," Gabrielle said as she headed for the ladies' room.

Gabrielle pushed open the door and saw Alyssa leaning against the old, white porcelain sink, her head in her hands. When Alyssa heard the door close again she lowered her hands. "Did he leave?" she asked softly.

Gabrielle nodded. "Yes. I just saw him pull out of the parking lot with Mike Bibbit and Nat Farrell."

"Those guys deserve each other," Alyssa said bitterly. She turned to face the sink, ran the cold water, and splashed some on her face. "I hope they'll all be very happy together."

Megan slipped into the bathroom and smiled sheepishly at Gabrielle. "Boy, Alyssa," she said. "That must have been some fight you had with Brock."

Alyssa grabbed a paper towel and dabbed at her forehead and cheeks. "Yes, it was."

"What are you going to do?" Gabrielle asked gently.

"I *was* going to catch the bus back to Leesville but I checked the bus schedule posted outside the ladies' room. It's already come and gone." Alyssa stared down into the sink.

"What about your parents?" Megan asked. "Can't they come get you?"

"They've gone to New York for the weekend." Alyssa gave a short, dry laugh. "Everything is just one, big mess."

Gabrielle stepped closer to Alyssa. "You could ride with us to Coconut Beach—"

"It would give you time to think everything through," Megan finished.

Alyssa dried her hands with the paper towel. She seemed to be considering the idea.

"And I'll bet that by the time we get to Coconut Beach," Megan continued enthusiastically, "Brock will have cooled off. Then you two will make up, and everything will be perfect again." Megan grinned as if all of Alyssa's problems were solved.

"But what if it isn't perfect?" Alyssa asked quietly. She picked up her bags and walked toward the door of the bathroom. "No, I think it's best if I just wait in the restaurant for tomorrow's bus."

"You want to stay *here*?" Megan asked, following Alyssa out of the bathroom. "Overnight? By yourself?" A few remaining students were standing in line by the cash register. Besides them, there was no one in the café except a few regulars, mostly tired truck drivers. "Staying here will only make you more miserable."

"I agree," Gabrielle whispered from behind Megan.

Alyssa looked around the now gloomy café. "But what else can I do?"

Megan and Gabrielle turned to look at each other. And when Gabrielle spoke, she spoke for both of them.

"Alyssa, if things don't work out with Brock once we get to Coconut Beach, you can stay with us at Aunt Kate's."

"Who's Aunt Kate?" Alyssa asked.

"You haven't heard of Aunt Kate?" Megan feigned shock. "She's only the most happening nurse ever to hit Coconut Beach."

Gabrielle rolled her eyes and laughed. "Well, I don't know about that. But her condo *is* right on the beach. And she has a spare room and a fold-out couch. There's enough room for all of us."

Alyssa chewed nervously on her lower lip. If things didn't work out with Brock once she got to Coconut Beach, she'd be stuck spending ten long days with two girls she scarcely knew.

Megan, the overly perky cheerleader, was so crazy and wild, and Gabrielle, with her artsy black clothes, was so—so *different*. Not that Alyssa was a snob; just that for the past four years she'd spent most of her time with Brock and his family. Lately, whenever she had thought of what her life would be like without Brock, she had come up with "lonely." Now that it looked as if she might actually be facing the possibility of life without Brock, she found herself not alone at all. Two girls who were virtual strangers were offering her their friendship. She'd be crazy not to accept.

"All right," Alyssa said finally. "I'll at least ride with you to Coconut Beach. But if things don't work out with Brock, I'm heading back to Leesville, locking myself in my bedroom, and having a *really* good cry!"

Gabrielle put her hand on Alyssa's shoulder, and Megan shook Alyssa's hand. "It's a deal."

The red Mustang convertible sped down the highway, and a warm breeze tossed the girls' hair. Gabrielle glanced at Alyssa, who sat in the bucket seat next to her. "Are you okay?"

Alyssa smiled. Her eyes were still red from crying. "Much better, thanks."

Megan leaned forward. "Isn't fate weird?" she said. "Only a few days ago Gabby and I were each going to be spending spring break all alone in Leesville. Then I crash into her car, and Alyssa and Brock have a fight, and boom!" She popped her sunglasses down on her nose and giggled. "We're all spending our vacation together!"

"Well, it was a bit more complicated than that for me," Gabrielle pointed out.

Alyssa sighed. "And even more complicated for me. Only a few days ago my life was all planned out for me. Everyone thought I was going to marry Brock, go to the University of Georgia, and live happily ever after." She smiled bravely. "And up until a few months ago, even I thought that's exactly what I'd be doing. I never thought we'd end *this* way. . . ."

"Oh, come on," Megan said as she squeezed Alyssa's shoulder. "You and Brock will get back together. You'll get married, go to the University of Georgia, and live happily ever after, just like it was supposed to happen."

"I'm not so sure about that." Alyssa twisted the promise ring encircling her finger. "I'm not sure about anything anymore."

Gabrielle pushed her dark, windswept hair off her forehead. "We hardly know each other, Alyssa, so I don't mean to interfere. But I'd say, go slowly. You're really young. You have plenty of time to get married."

"I've been trying to go slow," Alyssa replied, "but Brock, and his family, and my family, and even the kids at school, keep pushing me toward the altar. My mother is the worst. She got married right after high school and she's had a very happy marriage. Naturally, she wants the same for me. *And,* she has dreams of throwing the biggest wedding celebration Leesville's ever seen."

"My parents feel just the opposite," Megan

said. She popped a few corn chips in her mouth. "If I go out with a guy more than three times, they're afraid I'm getting too serious."

"Three times?" Gabrielle laughed a bit ruefully. "That would be a record for me."

Alyssa turned toward Gabrielle. "Haven't you dated much?"

Gabrielle pursed her lips. "Let's see. I went out once with Heath Perkins, the math teacher's son. But only because my dad asked me to do it as a favor to him. He was hoping to get a date with Mrs. Perkins."

Megan giggled. "So did he?"

"Yes." Gabrielle shook her head. "But he decided that Mrs. Perkins was just as strange as Perkins Junior, so we called it quits on the Perkins family."

"Was that your only date?" Alyssa asked politely.

"No, but the others were about as exciting. I don't know. Maybe I'm just one of those girls who doesn't hit her dating stride until college. I just wasn't having any luck with high school guys so I decided to give up on dating."

"I could never do that," Megan declared. "Dating is too much fun."

"Fun?" Gabrielle had to stop herself from turning around to gape at Megan. "I think it's agony! I mean, let's consider the average date.

First you get in a car with someone you hardly know and immediately have to decide between turning on the radio or making dumb small talk to fill the silence. Then you get to a restaurant and have to order dinner. Here's the tough part. Spaghetti's out—it has a life of its own. The last thing you want is tomato sauce all over your clothes."

Megan laughed. "Tacos are out, too. You bite one end and the stuffing shoots out the other end, right into your lap!"

"I think fried chicken is the worst," Alyssa confessed with a giggle. "I feel like such a slob eating it."

Gabrielle laughed. "But then you order something simple like a salad. . . ."

"And it's even more of a nightmare!" Alyssa finished.

"Particularly when the lettuce hasn't been cut up," Gabrielle added. "You take a forkful, thinking you'll get it all in your mouth, and surprise! There you are with lovely green foliage stuck to your face."

Megan fell back against the seat. "That settles it. I'm never going on a dinner date again. It's too dangerous."

"Hey, I think we're getting close," Gabrielle said excitedly. She took a deep breath. "You can smell the salt water in the air."

Each girl inhaled deeply. The air felt warmer and there was a slight edge of saltiness to it. Even the scenery had changed, from clusters of tall pines, to a sparse collection of scrubby vegetation.

Alyssa closed her eyes and leaned back against her seat. "It's wonderful, isn't it? It makes me feel peaceful."

"Umm," Megan agreed distractedly. "It makes *me* think of sun, surf, and boys."

"Everything makes you think of boys," Gabrielle cracked.

Megan leaned over the front seat. "What's wrong with that?"

"Nothing," Gabrielle answered quickly. She wasn't about to ruin her good mood by arguing with Megan Becker about a topic as silly as boys.

"I don't believe you think nothing is wrong with my thinking of boys all the time," Megan protested. "What about you, Alyssa? You must think a lot about boys."

"Well, not really. I mean, I think about Brock, of course." Alyssa tucked a strand of hair behind her ear and looked out at the low bushes bordering the highway. "Actually, I don't know all that much about boys."

"Ha!" Megan snorted. "That's a good one. You're the only one in this car who's ever had a steady boyfriend. You know more about boys than Gabby and me put together."

Alyssa turned to look at the other two girls. Even though her heart was torn by what had happened earlier with Brock, she actually felt good being with Gabrielle and Megan. In fact, she couldn't remember when she'd last spent time alone with girls her own age—that is, girls who weren't members of Brock's large family.

"Can I tell you both something?" Alyssa asked impulsively. "And would you promise not to tell a single soul?"

"Who am I going to tell?" Megan laughed bitterly. "No one on the squad is speaking to me!"

"Sure, Alyssa," Gabrielle added.

"I want your solemn promise that what I'm about to tell you won't leave this car," Alyssa continued seriously.

"Promise," Gabrielle and Megan answered simultaneously.

"Brock is the only boy I've ever kissed. I've never even held hands with another boy."

Only the fact that Gabrielle was driving kept her from staring at Alyssa in amazement. Here was Leesville's Homecoming Queen, first runner-up for state Junior Miss, and the envy of every girl in Leesville, Georgia—and she had only kissed one boy.

"I never really had the opportunity," Alyssa continued. "I've been going out with Brock since we were freshmen."

Megan gave Alyssa's shoulder another squeeze. "It's time you started living. As soon as we get to Gabrielle's aunt's house, we'll put on our bikinis. . . ."

"I don't have a bikini," Alyssa cut in. "And anyway, I'm not so sure I'm ready to start 'living.' Nothing's settled with Brock."

"Yeah, Megan," Gabrielle added. "I think Alyssa needs some time to think before she joins you on a major boy hunt!"

"Well, all right. But when you're ready, Alyssa, and you too, Gabrielle, I'll be your personal guide to the boys of Coconut Beach."

"What makes you such an expert?" Gabrielle asked.

"I read the papers," Megan replied matter-of-factly. "Every year about twenty-five thousand kids converge on Coconut Beach. Twenty thousand of them are guys."

"Twenty thousand," Alyssa gasped.

"Of course, they're all for the taking," Megan continued. "If you want a brown-haired guy with sea-green eyes and a tattoo on his chest that says 'Be Mine,' you can have him." Megan snapped her fingers. "Like that."

Gabrielle snorted. "Boys are people, too, you

know Megan. You talk about them as if they were pieces of fruit, ripe for the plucking!"

"Well, that's one way to put it!" Megan grinned, clearly undisturbed by Gabrielle's comment.

Alyssa laughed nervously. "And to think I was on my way to Brock's grandmother's house."

"That was two hours ago, in a whole other lifetime." Megan leaned forward excitedly. "Trust me. This spring break is going to change our lives!"

As if to protest Megan's assertion, the Mustang suddenly sputtered and coughed.

"What's the matter?" Alyssa asked.

"I don't know." Gabrielle glanced at the dashboard. A red warning light was glowing on the instrument panel. "But I'll have to pull over."

Gabrielle steered the Mustang over to the shoulder of the highway where it lurched to a stop.

Gabrielle swiped the drops of sweat from her face with the back of her arm and stood up straight again. "It's an oil leak."

"How do you know so much about cars?" Megan asked.

Gabrielle wiped her hands on a rag she had taken from the trunk. "Listen. This car belonged to my mother. When she died, my dad didn't have the heart to sell it so he saved it for me. It means a lot to me." Gabrielle sighed and slammed the hood shut. "You know, Megan, when you plowed into me the other day, I almost couldn't bear to see the damage. I still can't believe my dad was so calm about the accident."

Megan kicked the gravel with her sneaker. "Yeah, well, I wish my dad had been as calm. *I* still can't believe he let me go on this trip after the way he screamed and yelled."

Alyssa laughed. "I'm sorry, Megan. It's just that the whole thing is so absurd. First your accident, then my fight with Brock, now the car breaking down. . . ."

"Which brings us back to the problem at hand," Gabrielle said. She reached into the car, opened the glove compartment, and pulled out a map. "Did anyone notice the name of the last town we drove through?"

"Gilroy," Alyssa answered. "Right here." She pointed to a small mark on the map.

"And that was at least twenty minutes ago," Gabrielle said, looking up and down the long, empty stretch of highway and frowning. "We're about thirteen miles from Coconut Beach." She traced the blue line of the interstate with her finger and smiled ruefully. "And I don't see any gas stations looming on the horizon, do you?"

Alyssa shook her head. "No."

"It's too bad we were the last in the convoy," Megan added. "They probably haven't even noticed we're not with them anymore."

"Well, there's no use in complaining. We've got to do something," Gabrielle said firmly.

Megan walked over to the edge of the road and stuck out her thumb. "I say we hitchhike."

"I don't think that's such a good idea, Megan," Alyssa said nervously. "Do you know what happens to girls who hitchhike?"

"They meet interesting people," Megan said matter-of-factly.

"Interesting murderers," Alyssa replied.

"Come on, Alyssa. You're exaggerating." Megan peered down the road for prospective rides.

"Well, count me out." Alyssa walked back to the car and slid into the front seat. "I'd rather wait for a policeman."

Gabrielle was torn. The afternoon light was fading rapidly. If a highway patrol car didn't come before sundown, they could be in big trouble, stranded alone on a dark road. On the other hand, accepting a ride from total strangers was just too dangerous. Finally, Gabrielle sighed. "I'm with Alyssa."

"What!" Megan cried.

"Look, we'll wait just a little longer," Gabrielle argued. "We're only thirteen miles from Coconut Beach. A patrol car is bound to come by."

"That's just great!" Megan threw her arms in the air in exasperation. "We'll be stuck here until the end of spring break. I don't know about you guys, but I haven't counted very many patrol cars whizzing by. In fact, I haven't counted many cars of any kind. I say we flag down the next car and get out of here!"

"You haven't changed a bit, Megan!"

Gabrielle ran her hand through her hair in frustration. "When we were little kids, you were always jumping into things without considering the consequences!"

"At least I *did* things," Megan retorted. "If you'd had your way, we wouldn't have done anything."

Gabrielle turned to Alyssa, still sitting in the car, as if to appeal to her. "Our parents told us never, ever to go swimming in the old rock quarry. Of course, Megan decided that meant we *had* to go swimming in the old rock quarry."

"It was a good idea," Megan said stoutly. "The water was cold and it was surrounded by big rocks just perfect for diving."

"Sure. The water was cold and the rocks were perfect. But tell Alyssa what else the quarry held."

"Just a few alligators." Megan shrugged. "No big deal."

"No big deal! They were over six feet long! Some kids had thrown them into the quarry when they were still tiny," Gabrielle explained. "If a guard hadn't spotted us just as we were about to dive in, we would have been dinner for a hungry alligator family."

Megan rolled her eyes. "You've always been a stick in the mud, Gabby. What about the time we went to the amusement park and I wanted to ride the Sea Serpent roller coaster?" Now it was Megan's turn to appeal to Alyssa. "Miss Excitement refused."

"I felt sick," Gabrielle protested. "I'd eaten two corn dogs and a mound of cotton candy."

"You didn't ride because you were scared," Megan said flatly. She crossed her arms over her chest and glared at Gabrielle, who returned the glare evenly.

Alyssa cleared her throat. "If you don't mind my asking, when did these particular incidents occur?"

"When we were in third grade," Gabrielle replied quickly.

"Nine years ago," Alyssa pointed out. "Why are you still arguing?"

"We're not arguing," Gabrielle corrected her. "I was merely using the alligator episode as an example of how looking before you leap can save you from a lot of trouble."

Megan tossed her head. "And I was merely using the roller coaster episode as an example of how you never want to have any fun."

"I have fun," Gabrielle replied hotly. "It's just that your kind of fun and my kind of fun aren't the same."

"They used to be." Megan allowed a small smile to soften her expression. "Remember the time we built the piñata for our Brownie troop?

You painted its face to look exactly like our troop leader, Mrs. Mardoff."

Gabrielle couldn't help but smile. They had almost gotten kicked out the troop for that prank.

"And remember the time we entered Miss Amelia in the 4th of July pet contest?"

Gabrielle nodded. "And we dressed her up like a little old lady for the Best Dressed Pet Division."

Megan grinned. "Miss Amelia got loose and Shannon Dobbler's poodle ran after her. Next thing you know, every dog in the contest had joined in the chase. The judges had to cancel the entire contest!"

Alyssa had been listening to Gabrielle and Megan's reminiscences a bit enviously. "You know, I grew up in Leesville, but I don't remember alligators in the quarry, or the 4th of July pet contest. Where was I when you two were having so much fun?"

"Dating Brock," Gabrielle and Megan chorused.

"At the age of nine?"

"Well, you did go to a different school. I guess you moved with a different crowd," Gabrielle suggested.

"And the whole time you were just waiting to meet us and really start to live," Megan joked.

"And speaking of waiting, I'm getting a little tired of doing just that. Everyone else is already in Coconut Beach and we're stuck here on an abandoned highway!"

Gabrielle blew the bangs off her forehead. "Well, if you're so upset, do something useful. And I don't mean stick out your thumb."

"All right, I will." Megan walked over to the Mustang, reached into the back seat, and pulled out her nylon bag. She slung it over her shoulder and stuck her visor on her head.

"What are you doing?" Gabrielle asked suspiciously.

"You said to do something useful, and I am. I'm going to walk to Coconut Beach, find a mechanic, and send him back here."

But before Megan could begin her hike, the girls heard the not-too-distant roar of an engine. In a moment, they spotted a sleek, red BMW approaching. In another moment, it had pulled up behind Gabrielle's Mustang.

"Megan," Gabrielle whispered, "that car has stopped."

Megan arched her eyebrows. "Really? I hadn't noticed."

"And there are two boys in the front seat," Alyssa whispered.

"Oh, and of course I hadn't noticed *that*! What's wrong with you two?"

73

Gabrielle stood tensely as the passenger in the red BMW rolled down his window and leaned out. His dark hair was tousled and a pair of mirrored sunglasses were perched on his nose.

"Hey, you girls need a lift?" he called.

"No, thank you," Gabrielle called back.

Ignoring her friend's hesitancy, Megan sauntered back to the car. "Where are you boys headed?"

The driver, a sunbleached blond with a deep tan, leaned out of his window. "Coconut Beach. How about you?"

"Chad!" Megan cried, grinning broadly. "Remember me? I'm Megan Becker. I'm on the cheerleading team at Leesville High with your cousin Leslie."

Chad smiled knowingly. "Ah, yes. Becker the Wrecker. If I remember correctly, you totaled your car right in front of our fraternity house."

"Hey, I was there when it happened," the dark-haired boy added. "We were playing touch football on the TKE lawn."

Megan blushed. "I didn't actually *total* the car."

"Whatever. Anyway, looks like you've got car trouble again."

The dark-haired boy flipped up his mirrored sunglasses and Megan thought she'd faint. He had the most startling blue eyes she'd ever seen. There was no way she'd let these boys drive away without her!

"If it's not too much trouble," Megan asked, "would you mind giving us a lift into Coconut Beach?"

"Of course not," Chad replied. He nodded toward Gabrielle. "But your friend there said you didn't need a ride."

Megan grinned. "Never mind her. I'll be right back."

Megan hurried up to the Mustang. "This is too perfect," she whispered to Gabrielle and Alyssa. "Two gorgeous guys from Georgia Tech just dying to come to the rescue of three stranded girls!"

Gabrielle rolled her eyes. "How well do you know these guys, Megan?"

"I met Chad at Leslie Harrington's house last Christmas. The other guy obviously knows *me*!"

Alyssa looked back at the BMW warily. "I still don't feel comfortable getting into a car with strange boys."

"And I don't feel comfortable leaving my car," Gabrielle said.

Megan looked at her companions as if they had just betrayed her to her worst enemy. "I can't believe you guys," she said. "Two perfectly polite college boys, one of them Leslie Harrington's cousin, have offered to give us a ride into Coconut Beach. What possible objection can you have now?"

Gabrielle had to admit the boys did seem harmless enough. And they'd yet to spot a patrol car. If they accepted a ride into Coconut Beach, she could ask them to drop her off at the first gas station they came to, where she'd arrange for a tow truck to retrieve the Mustang.

"All right," Gabrielle said. "Alyssa, I think it's probably the best thing to do at this point."

Alyssa nodded. "I'll go with them. But I'm still not happy about it."

"Hey, girls!" Chad shouted. "I don't want to rush you, but the longer we spend on this highway, the less time we spend partying tonight. You know what I mean?"

"We know," Gabrielle called back. She set about fastening the Mustang's convertible top. Then she retrieved their suitcases from the trunk and the back seat, and double-checked the locks.

"Hey, you don't have to be so nervous about the car," the dark-haired boy called. "If it's broken down, no one's going to steal it!"

Gabrielle ignored his comment, then took the note Alyssa had written to the highway police and stuck it securely behind one of the windshield wipers.

The dark-haired boy got out of the BMW and flashed the three girls a smile made for a toothpaste ad. "I'm Jason. And this is Chad."

Megan introduced Gabrielle and Alyssa. "And I'm Megan," she added, fluttering her eyelashes in what she hoped was an appealing way.

Gabrielle and Megan climbed into the back seat of the BMW. Alyssa hung back for a moment. Here she was getting into a car with two college boys who were virtually strangers. Brock would be furious if he knew.

"There's room for you up front," Chad said, gesturing to the empty passenger seat. "Slide in."

Alyssa shook herself out of her reverie and saw that Jason had gotten into the back seat with Gabrielle and Megan. Without a word she scooted onto the black leather seat and closed the door.

"All right, buddy, put the pedal to the metal," Jason cried. "We're outta here!"

Chad laughed and pressed the accelerator to the floor. The BMW sped back onto the highway with a spray of gravel.

Once they were cruising down the highway, Megan turned to Jason. "So, where are you guys staying?" she asked brightly.

"At the Flamingo."

"That's great!" Megan exclaimed. "All my friends are staying there."

"What are Alyssa and I?" Gabrielle asked with false cheer. "Your chauffeur and chaperon?"

Megan laughed brightly. "Oh, Gabby, don't be silly. You know what I mean." She turned to Jason. "The rest of my cheerleading squad is staying at the Flamingo. The three of us are staying at Gabrielle's aunt's condo." Megan paused. "You know, tomorrow night the whole crowd from Leesville High is going to a crab feast on Porter's Island. It should be a blast."

"Then you'll be there?" Jason asked.

Megan nodded. "Of course. I wouldn't miss it."

"Maybe we'll drop by," he said casually. "You know, just check out the action."

Megan discreetly poked Gabrielle's leg. "That would be fabulous," she replied, with another flutter of her eyelashes.

While Jason and Megan chatted, and Gabrielle stared out at the passing scenery, Chad continued to steal quick looks at Alyssa. Finally, he cleared his throat.

"Hey, Alyssa, ever since you got into the car, I've been thinking I've seen you before."

From the back seat Jason groaned loudly. "Now *that*'s an original line if I've ever heard one."

"No, I'm serious," Chad continued. "I know I've seen you before."

Alyssa smiled shyly but didn't answer.

"Well, if you were in Leesville for Homecoming by any chance, you might have seen Alyssa in the parade. She was our queen," Megan told him.

"That's it," Chad said excitedly. And then the smile faded from his face. "I seem to remember my cousin Leslie tell me the Homecoming Queen was going out with Leesville's halfback, Brock Jorgensen."

"Well, yes, that was . . . I mean is, true," Alyssa answered. She had no desire to tell a complete stranger about her problems with Brock.

"It figures." Chad sighed dramatically. "Every beautiful girl has a boyfriend."

These guys are too much, Gabrielle thought angrily. First she had to spend one leg of the drive with jocks Mike Bibbit and Nat Farrell. Now she had to be with these college jerks.

"How much longer?" Gabrielle asked.

Chad pointed out the window. "There's the bridge over the sound. Coconut Beach is just on the other side."

Megan giggled. "I can't wait!"

Alyssa gazed out at the long, low bridge. She was glad to have something to focus on other than what was happening in the car. The bridge arched over a broad, swampy area that gave way to a stand of cypress trees, and then again to an area of swamp. It seemed strange to be visiting a new place without Brock at her side. Strange, but exciting. For four years they had done everything, gone everywhere together. She was sure spring break was going to be an unbelievable adventure.

The BMW drove onto the bridge at exactly seven o'clock. As it approached the center, a neat, white sign announced, "Welcome to Coconut Beach." The BMW cruised past the sign and over the crest of the bridge. The girls let out a collective gasp.

Spread out before them was a long string of

lights bordering a great arc of white, sandy beach. Blinking neon signs cast a pink and green glow over the bustling road ahead. The signs, shaped like palm trees, flamingos, giant fish, and alligators, advertised the best pizza, the hottest live music, and the cheapest overnight rates.

"I didn't think Coconut Beach was this big. Or this bright," Alyssa said as she looked around in amazement.

"It looks like one big amusement park," Megan added, as she leaned over Jason to get a better view.

"It looks like a madhouse." Gabrielle looked in dismay as a long line of red taillights snaked out ahead of them. "The traffic is bumper to bumper."

Jason nodded. "The Flamingo is less than a half a mile from here and it'll probably take us thirty minutes to get there."

"Pull over at the first service station, Chad," Gabrielle instructed. She glanced at her watch. She couldn't bear to think of what would happen to her Mustang if it spent the night alone on the highway.

"Right." Chad eased the BMW into the parade of cars inching slowly down the strip. From the little they could see, most of the cars sported out of town plates and were loaded with high school and college kids and their vacation gear. Horns honked, voices shouted, and radios blared as the drivers jockeyed for a place in line.

Gabrielle stared incredulously at the crowds streaming along the sidewalks. She had never seen so many people her own age gathered in one place.

"I can't believe we're here!" Megan squealed, bouncing lightly on the seat. "Ten solid days of fun and sun!"

She forgot boys, Gabrielle thought with a wry smile.

Jason grinned at Megan indulgently. "Hey, chill. You're going to give yourself a heart attack."

"Oh, don't worry about that. I can take an awful lot of excitement," she replied coyly.

Gabrielle interrupted their flirtation. "There's a service station up on the left. You can drop us off there, Chad." She could see a green pick-up with a winch and small crane on its flatbed in the station's lot.

When he reached the station, Chad signaled and turned into the lot. As he crossed the pedestrian walk, several girls in bikini tops and shorts turned back to look admiringly at the shiny, red BMW. One of them called to Chad. "Cool car."

Chad grinned and waved. "Well, girls. Here we are."

Alyssa felt enormous relief; she couldn't wait

to get out of Chad's car. Just sitting beside a boy who wasn't Brock was making her uncomfortable. Gabrielle was just as relieved to take her leave of Chad and his friend. Now she could arrange to have her Mustang brought into Coconut Beach in one piece. Only Megan was sorry to get out of the BMW. She'd found two really cute guys before she'd even gotten to Coconut Beach and she wasn't too happy about letting them get away.

"So, will I see you again?" she asked Jason as she put her hand lightly on his arm.

"Probably." Jason shrugged. "It's a small town."

Chad turned to Alyssa. "We'll be hanging out at Dune Buggies tonight. Why don't you be there, too?"

"I really don't . . . what's Dune Buggies, anyway?"

Megan sighed in exasperation. "It's only *the* most 'in' under twenty-one club in Coconut Beach. Everyone who's anyone hangs out there."

"Megan, the Coconut Beach expert," Gabrielle added with a laugh.

"Is there dancing?" Alyssa asked impulsively. She hadn't danced in such a long time. Brock hated to dance and only agreed to slow dance at formals, like Homecoming or a prom.

"Dancing, eating, drinking, whatever." Chad leaned toward her earnestly. "So? Will I see you tonight?"

Alyssa twisted the promise ring on her finger. Before she could say a word, Megan blurted out, "Don't worry. We'll be there."

Gabrielle cleared her throat. "I hate to remind you guys, but we have to do something about my car before we go anywhere tonight. Like, get it towed."

Megan turned to Jason. "If for some reason we don't make it tonight, remember the crab feast on Porter's Island tomorrow night. You can buy a ticket at the pier."

The three girls got out of the car. As Chad pulled away, Megan waved and called after them. "See you tonight!"

Gabrielle tugged on Megan's arm. "Come on. We've got to get my car towed and then get ourselves to my aunt's house."

"Well, why don't you give me her address, and I'll meet you both there later."

"Oh, no you don't!" Gabrielle said as she shook her head. "We're all in this together. My dad told your dad I'd take you to my aunt's house, and that's exactly what I'm going to do. After that, you can follow Jason to Timbuktu."

Gabrielle headed toward the station. "I'm going to talk to the mechanic, then call my aunt. Alyssa, don't let Megan out of your sight."

Megan stuck her tongue out at Gabrielle. "Party pooper."

Megan and Alyssa sat down by the pumps to wait. After a few minutes they saw a man get into the tow truck and pull away. Gabrielle rejoined them.

"Well, the mechanic won't be able to work on my car until Monday. At least they sent someone to tow it in." She plopped down beside Megan and Alyssa.

"Bummer," Megan said sympathetically.

"What's worse is my aunt's working overtime at the hospital tonight. She won't be able to pick us up until nine o'clock."

"Are you kidding?" Megan asked. "That's fantastic!"

"What's fantastic about sitting in a service station for two hours?"

Megan shook her head in amazement. "Gabby, you really are incredible. Why would you imagine we'd sit here watching the traffic lights change, when we could spend the next couple of hours having fun?"

"Well," Alyssa said as she stood up. "I could go for something to eat."

"And I know just the place. Dune Buggies!"

Megan stood up and draped her arm around Alyssa's shoulder.

"So that you can find Jason?" Gabrielle asked with a grin.

"Of course. And so that Alyssa can get something to eat. And so that you . . . well, you can do whatever you want when we get there. How about it?"

Dune Buggie's stood apart from the other nightclubs along the beach. A gigantic red-and-white striped tent had been erected on an old wooden pier. Tiny white lights lined the wooden railings bordering the open-air dance floor stretching far out over the water.

"It looks like a circus," Alyssa said.

They neared the disco, and as Megan heard the pounding music, she broke into a trot. She couldn't wait to join the party.

The entrance ramp was lined with flashing neon signs in the shape of pointing hands. Signs inside the hands said things like, "This is the place!" and "Party On!" Alyssa and Gabrielle clambered up the wooden planks and came to stand behind Megan, who was waiting for them at the top. "This is even more incredible than I'd imagined," she gasped.

The vast dance floor was swarming with kids moving to music that pounded from gigantic speaker columns positioned along the edges of the pier. A deejay dressed as a lifeguard sat atop a tall lifeguard's station, complete with a built-in console. Colorful food stands sold hot dogs, tacos, burgers, and fries, and tables with striped umbrellas were grouped on multi-level wooden platforms.

"This isn't a circus. It's a zoo!" Gabrielle corrected, as she was jostled by a guy hopping up and down and flapping his arms to the beat.

"Let's get something to drink," Alyssa shouted as they moved into the disco. "I'm thirsty."

Megan stood on tiptoe and spotted a circular bar in the center of the tent. "Follow me," she shouted back.

Megan pushed her way between two muscular guys who were bantering with a pretty blond bartender, and called back over her shoulder, "What do you say we splurge and have a Fruit Bomb?"

"What's that?" Gabrielle asked.

Megan read off the ingredients from a blackboard on a stand behind the bar. "Pineapple juice, orange juice, and Seven-Up, topped with an orange slice and a cherry."

"I think that would make me throw up!" Gabrielle grimaced. "I'll just have a diet soda."

"I'll have the same," Alyssa said. "A Fruit Bomb on an empty stomach . . . ugh!"

Megan was just about to shout her order when she heard a familiar voice. "Becker! Becker the Wrecker!"

Megan turned and spotted Tom Hooper making his way toward them through the crowd. Raising her eyes, she saw Shannon and the rest of the cheerleading squad sitting at a large table on a platform overlooking the dance floor. Shannon wore a neon-striped sundress and looked as if she had just stepped out of a fashion magazine.

"The entire Leesville convoy must have driven straight to Dune Buggies," Gabrielle remarked as Tom came up beside them. She had spotted Shannon and the others, too.

Alyssa ducked behind Gabrielle. "You don't see Brock, do you?"

Gabrielle looked up at Shannon's table. "He's not with Shannon. Mike Bibbit's there, though."

Alyssa was relieved. She was tired and hungry, and though a part of her badly wanted to make things right with Brock again, another part of her wanted to avoid him, at least for a while.

Alyssa nodded. "Good. Look, I don't know

about you, but I'm hungry. Why don't I get us some fries?"

"Good idea," Gabrielle said.

The moment Alyssa disappeared into the crowd, the air was split by a shrill whistle from the deejay in the lifeguard get-up. "Listen up, all you beach bunnies and bozos! The big hand is on the twelve," he announced through his microphone, "and the other hand is on your date. That means it must be—"

The majority of the crowd raised glasses and shouted, "Limbo time!"

"That's right. Let's have all the limber guys and girls line up on the dance floor. The contest is about to begin. And, folks, this is a special one. We call it 'Double or Nothing.' Guys, grab yourselves a Limbo girl, and give the chick a Limbo whirl."

Megan's stomach suddenly tightened in nervousness. For weeks before spring break she'd been telling everyone how good she was at the Limbo. But, as she'd admitted to her sister, Sara, she'd never actually *done* the Limbo. She couldn't even really remember why she'd lied to her friends in the first place. She guessed it had something to do with wanting to fit in, to be accepted by Shannon's crowd. Anyway, after the accident, she'd never had a chance to practice the Limbo, either alone or with the other cheerleaders. And now, here she was, facing a disco full of kids, including Shannon and her crowd, who, considering they were already mad at her, would really let her have it if she couldn't back up her boasting with a great performance.

"Aren't you going to enter?" Tom Hooper asked. He grabbed her arm and pushed her toward the growing line of contestants. "Come on, Megan, the glory of Leesville High depends on you!"

"I can't," Megan replied, panicked by her own lack of experience, and the growing line of eager contestants. "I don't have a partner."

Tom scanned the crowd hopefully. "Isn't there someone from the squad who could enter with you?"

Megan looked up at Shannon, who smiled down at her smugly. Megan steeled herself. She *had* to enter. If she didn't, Shannon would never let her live it down.

"Gabby!" Megan cried desperately. "Be my partner!"

"Are you out of your mind?" Gabrielle took a step back. "I haven't done a backbend in years."

"Yeah, but you used to be the most limber girl in gymnastics," Megan countered. "You could do a back walkover before anyone else could."

"But that was in seventh grade," Gabrielle

protested, as Megan reached for her arm. "You know what a klutz I am now."

Megan sighed in frustration. Gabrielle couldn't be convinced. Then she spotted a dark-haired boy with sparkling blue eyes standing at the edge of the part of the dance floor that had been roped off for the contest. "Jason!"

"Last call for contestants!" A guy in thongs, electric blue shorts, and an orange, muscle T-shirt was counting off each team as they entered the ring. He jerked his thumb toward Megan. "Are you in or out?"

Megan glanced up at Shannon once more, then back at Jason. "We're in!" she declared. Megan grabbed Gabrielle's hand and dragged her into the ring.

The guy in the orange T-shirt refastened the rope, and the deejay announced, "With these last two Limbo lovelies, we're ready to go!" The crowd whooped and shouted as a spotlight focused momentarily on Gabrielle and Megan. "Let the contest begin!"

Megan could make out Tom Hooper's voice above the crowd's noise. "Go, Leesville!"

Gabrielle shut her eyes against the harsh light and ducked her head. "I don't want to do this," she hissed. "Let's get out of here, *now!*"

Megan gripped Gabrielle's arm tightly. "Please do this one favor for me," she pleaded.

"I promise I'll never ask you for another thing as long as I live."

"Megan!" Gabrielle protested. "I am *not* doing this!"

The speakers crackled with static, and then Chubby Checker began to sing.

"Here we go!" Megan watched as the first couple danced under the bamboo pole. Still holding tightly to Gabrielle's arm, Megan shuffled forward with the rest of the line.

"Let go of me, Megan!" Gabrielle tried to bolt over the rope, but several bystanders jokingly barred her way. She was caught. Gabrielle was horrified. She hated being in the spotlight, but it looked as if, at least for tonight, she'd have to play it Megan's way.

"How low can you go?" Chubby Checker asked and the crowd joined him. *"How low can you go?"* it roared.

"It's our turn!" The judges motioned Megan and Gabrielle toward the bamboo pole. "Come on, Gabby, this is an easy one."

The two girls slipped easily under the pole which was held at shoulder height.

"Are you happy?" Gabrielle asked as they scurried back to the end of the line to wait for their next turn.

"Thanks, Gabby." Megan's eyes shone. "I

have a confession to make. I've never actually done the Limbo before."

Gabrielle's eyes widened. "I can't believe you," she whispered. "I heard you promise Shannon Dobbler you'd teach everyone the Limbo. Why did you lie to her?"

Megan looked away hastily. "Well, it's, uh, it's a long story. But it doesn't matter now. Come on, it's our turn again."

Megan and Gabrielle again slid under the Limbo pole with relative ease. But when their third turn approached, Gabrielle wasn't sure she could make it.

"I don't know, Megan," she said. "The pole is awfully low. I think I'm going to let you down."

"No, you won't. Come on!"

"Wait!" Gabrielle cried. The girls leaned backward and Megan made her way under the pole. But Gabrielle whacked her forehead against it. There was an audible gasp from the crowd as Gabrielle staggered backward and fell down hard on the wooden floor. She rubbed her forehead ruefully as the spectators burst out laughing.

"Awwww, toooooo bad!" The deejay jerked his thumb like an umpire and bellowed, "You're outta there!"

Megan hurried back to Gabrielle and helped her to stand. "Are you okay?"

"No, I am not okay. I'm mortified. I told you I couldn't do the Limbo!"

The girls walked out of the roped area. "Come on, Gabby," Megan said as she put her arm around her friend's shoulder. "It was only a game."

Gabrielle shrugged off Megan's arm. "Yes, I know. But sometimes I think that's what everything is to you. A game."

Gabrielle knew she was being unfair to Megan. Well, she'd apologize to her later. Right now she needed something to drink, and maybe some ice for her forehead. Gabrielle pushed her way into the crowd. Megan started to follow but a tall figure stepped in her path. It was Jason. He folded his arms across his chest and declared, "I just lost five dollars."

Megan shook her head. "What do you mean?"

"I lost it on a bet."

"A bet?"

"Yeah. I bet the other TKEs that you would win the Limbo contest."

"Oh." Megan's smile brightened. "We *could* have won it," she said, "but Gabby's heart wasn't really in it." Jason looked at her intently, a bemused smile on his face. Megan blushed. "Sorry about your losing the money," she added.

"That's okay," he replied easily. "I know a way you can make it up to me."

"How?" Megan's heart raced with anticipation.

"Take a walk with me on the beach and we'll call it even."

Megan could feel herself blush again. One of the most gorgeous guys she had ever met had just asked her to take a moonlight walk on the beach.

"Sure," she giggled. "I mean, yes. I mean, when?"

"How about now?" Jason slipped his arm around her waist and a row of goosebumps raced up Megan's bare arm. Before she really knew what was happening, he was guiding her toward the nearest exit.

As they moved through the crowd, a tiny voice in the back of her head told Megan she should find Alyssa or Gabrielle first and tell them where she was going. But she was afraid that Jason might change his mind. Megan took a deep breath and let the handsome boy lead her down the ramp toward the beach.

Alyssa stood on tiptoe and searched the crowd
for Megan and Gabrielle. She had made the mis-
take of ordering a plate of fries and one of
nachos for the three of them to share. She had
no idea the servings would be so huge. In her
right hand, a long plastic boat piled high with
fries balanced precariously. In her left hand, a
plate of hot, gooey nachos threatened to fall to
the floor.

"Need some help with those?"

Alyssa turned to see who had spoken and
found herself staring directly into a pair of dark,
brown eyes. There was something vaguely familiar about them, she thought.

Then their owner smiled, revealing the tiny
dimple in his right cheek, and Alyssa cried,
"You're the boy from Carter's Truck Stop!"

The plastic boat tipped and several fries slid

to the floor. The boy quickly took the boat from her hand. "And you're the girl who drops things."

Alyssa blushed. She had been crying when they'd met earlier. She must have looked awful. "I'm sorry about this afternoon. I was terribly upset."

"There's nothing to apologize for. How are you feeling now?" The boy lifted the boat of fries over his head and led Alyssa toward a small empty table at the far side of the tent.

"Much better, thanks." Alyssa placed the plate of nachos on the table.

"I'm glad." The boy set the fries down beside the nachos and grinned. "I don't mean to be rude, but this is a lot of food for one person."

"Oh, it's not just for me." Alyssa laughed. She flipped her hair over her shoulders and looked out over the crowd once more for Gabrielle and Megan. "It's for my . . ." Alyssa's voice trailed off, then she whispered, "Oh, no."

"What is it?"

Alyssa panicked. Brock had just come into Dune Buggies and was scanning the crowd. Alyssa knew she couldn't face him here, in the loud, crazy disco. She turned to the boy. "Hide me!" she demanded.

He raised his eyebrows in surprise, then

looked quickly around for a suitable hiding place. "How about over there?" He pointed to a bright green canvas cabana which served as a telephone booth.

Alyssa raced for the small tent, ducked inside, and pulled the flap shut behind her. Her heart pounded as she pulled back the tent flap a bit and peeked through the narrow opening. The boy was standing just outside.

"Could you stand there for a few minutes?" she asked him.

He shrugged good-naturedly. "Sure." He turned to face the room and tucked his hands in the pockets of his jeans. "Is there anything in particular I should be watching for?"

"It's not a *thing*," Alyssa said softly. "It's a person, and I'm not up to seeing him right now."

"Ah." The boy remained silent for a moment. Finally, he tugged on his earlobe and asked, "Is life with you always this exciting?"

Alyssa giggled nervously. "Actually, my life is very dull," she replied. "This has just been one of those days."

She cautiously opened the flap another few inches and watched Brock make his way to the center bar. She saw him look up to the platform and spot the kids from Leesville. After he had joined them on the platform, Alyssa shifted her gaze to the boy standing outside the booth. He was so close that Alyssa could smell his aftershave. It had a sharp, clean scent, like freshly cut limes. She followed the strong line of his profile with her eyes, and admired the long, straight nose and firm chin.

The boy sensed he was being watched and turned to meet her eyes. "Is the coast clear?" he asked.

Alyssa nodded and pushed the tent flap open. "I think so."

A popular song began and there was a great surge of people toward the dance floor. Alyssa liked the song, and wished she could join them.

Her face must have reflected her desire because the boy promptly asked her to dance.

"Yes," Alyssa said quickly. But when he held out his hand to escort her to the dance floor, she stepped back into the safety of the phone booth. "But I can't."

"You can't?"

Alyssa peered up at the Leesville table. Brock was still there. If she walked onto the dance floor, there was a good chance he would see her. And of course he'd then want to talk to her. "At least, not now."

The boy looked steadily at Alyssa. Then, he shrugged. "Well, I can wait." He checked his watch and smiled. "Dune Buggies is open until two A.M."

"What time is it now?" Alyssa asked.

"Almost nine," he replied.

"Oh, no!" Alyssa sprang from the booth and spun in a circle. She had to find the nearest exit. "No wonder I couldn't find Gabrielle and Megan," she exclaimed. "They've probably already gone." Alyssa put her hand on the boy's arm. "I know it's a lot to ask," she said, "and you've been so nice already. But would you do me one more favor?"

His eyes twinkled with amusement. "You're crazy, you know that?"

"Please!"

"I'm sorry. What do you want me to do?"

"Would you walk next to me? At least until I get outside. I don't want—"

"I know, I know," he cut in. "You don't want a certain someone to see you." He held out his arm and grinned. "This is getting more interesting by the second. Come on."

Alyssa and the boy stepped into the crowd and moved swiftly toward the nearest exit. Alyssa pressed herself against the boy's side, making sure to keep his body between her and Brock. They had almost reached the main ramp when Alyssa saw Monica Levitts come out of the ladies' room. She was headed right toward them.

"Put your arms around me, quick!" Alyssa ordered.

"What?"

Alyssa pulled his arms around her waist and buried her head in his chest. She expected at any second to hear Monica call her name. But nothing happened. After a moment, she lifted her head. The boy was staring down at her with the most peculiar expression. Suddenly, Alyssa was mortified.

"I—I'm so sorry. I really don't ever—I mean, this is not how I usually act. Please, believe me, I would never—"

"I believe you," he said softly. Then he leaned down and gently placed his lips against hers.

For a second, Alyssa was too startled to respond. She had never been kissed by any boy but Brock and she was surprised at how different it felt. She closed her eyes. His heart was pounding against her chest—or was it her own heart she felt? She couldn't tell. It was all so new and wonderful.

"Oh, my God!" Alyssa cried. "What am I doing?" She pulled herself away from him and stumbled toward the exit ramp.

"I'm sorry." The boy hurriedly followed her.

"I don't know why I did that." He shook his head. "What am I talking about? Yes, I do."

"It's okay," Alyssa cried. "But I've really got to go." She raced down the long wooden plank.

"Wait a minute," the boy shouted after her. "I don't even know your name."

"Alyssa," she called over her shoulder as she hurried away.

Megan and Jason stood alone, side by side at the water's edge, watching the waves roll onto the shore. The reflection of the town lights shimmered upon the glassy surface of the bay. The light breeze blowing off the gulf felt pleasantly warm against Megan's skin.

This was the moment Megan had been dreaming of since she'd met Jason earlier that day. But now that it was here, she couldn't think of a thing to say. Whatever topic came to mind, like cheerleading, or high school, suddenly seemed childish and immature. Finally, Megan decided she would ask Jason about life at Georgia Tech. She turned to look at him and found herself being stared at by his cool, blue eyes.

"What's the matter?" Megan asked self-consciously.

Jason tapped the tip of her nose with his finger. "You have the . . . the cutest nose." He grinned impishly. "It's those little freckles that do it."

Megan blushed with pleasure. "No one's ever told me that before."

"Well, you have," he replied as he put his arm around her waist. He leaned closer and nuzzled his face into her neck. "The water's nice, isn't it?"

Megan stiffened slightly at his touch. "Yes, it is," she answered lamely.

Jason slid his hands along her waist as he planted little kisses along her shoulders. "Your skin feels so soft," he rumbled in her ear. "I like that."

The places where he touched her tingled and shivered. Megan couldn't deny that she was enjoying his romantic attentions, but still she thought he was moving awfully fast. Suddenly, Megan felt terribly vulnerable, alone on the beach with a boy she barely knew. She slipped out of his arms and, leaving her sandals on the sand, skipped out into the shallows.

"It's just gorgeous out here," she called, splashing the water with her feet.

Jason stood at the water's edge and watched her for a moment. Then he laughed, kicked off his shoes, and waded in after her. "It is beautiful," he said, coming up beside her. "Just like you."

Megan shivered again.

"Why'd you run off like that?" he asked as he took her by the hand. "It might have given me the impression you don't like me."

"That's not true," Megan replied quickly. "It's just that—"

Jason pulled her toward him and held her tightly against his body. The water swirled around their ankles as he pressed his mouth against hers. There was an urgency to his kiss that frightened Megan. She tried to pull her head away but he only tightened his grip, cupping the back of her head in his hand and pushing her lips against his.

Megan put her hands against his chest and pushed him away. "Jason, slow down. We've only just met."

"What's the matter?" He laughed. "Afraid?"

"Of course not." Megan folded her arms across her chest. "I just think we should get to know each other first."

With a laugh, Jason scooped her up in his arms and waded up onto the shore.

"Wh-where are we going?" Megan asked in a shaky voice.

"Someplace where we can get better acquainted," he replied with a grin.

Megan knew she was in way over her head. She had to do something, and do it fast.

Megan clutched her stomach and bellowed. "Oh, no! Put me down, please!"

"What?" Jason was so startled he nearly dropped her on the sand. "What's the matter?"

"My stomach!" Megan moaned. "It hurts."

Jason settled her on the sand and knelt beside her. "Is it a stomach ache?"

"I think it's appendicitis."

"Where does it hurt?" Jason demanded. "On the right or left side?"

Megan tried to remember just where the appendix was located, but she couldn't. She hugged her middle and writhed back and forth across the sand. "Both."

"Both?" Jason sat back on his heels. "How bad is it?"

"Pretty bad," Megan groaned.

Jason licked his lips nervously. "I'd better go get a doctor."

He leaped to his feet and Megan screamed, "No!" He looked down at her in alarm and she added, more calmly, "Please, I—I just need to lie here for a while."

Jason put his hands on his hips. "Look, if it's really that bad, I should get some help."

Great, Megan thought. *What do I do now?* Pretending to be sick had seemed like a brilliant idea, but she hadn't thought of all it would entail. Like recovery.

Jason glanced down at his watch. "It's only nine-fifteen. Chad should still be at Dune Buggies. Why don't I run back and get him. We'll give you a ride to the emergency room."

"Nine-fifteen!" Megan yelped. She was supposed to meet Gabrielle and Alyssa at nine. Gabrielle was already upset with her. The last thing Megan wanted was for her to get any more upset.

Still, Megan didn't want Jason to know she was faking. She clutched her stomach again. "Jason, do you remember the service station you guys dropped us at earlier?"

He nodded. "I guess."

"Well, Gabby's aunt is supposed to meet us there right about now. She's a nurse. If you could just help me get there, she could take me to the hospital."

Relief washed over Jason's face. "Great. But do you think you can make it?"

"I—I think so," she gasped. Megan wasn't sure how a person with appendicitis was supposed to walk. She slowly stood up, leaned heavily on Jason's arm, and effected a limp.

Megan and Jason made their way back to the main road through town, and soon spotted the service station's glowing sign. They picked up their pace.

"It's not far now," Jason said.

Megan felt absolutely ridiculous. It was bad enough she had made such a fool of herself with Jason. She couldn't bear the thought of Gabrielle and Alyssa seeing her hobbling along next to the guy she'd sworn to win. They'd think she was one of those all talk, no action girls. Megan winced. She knew the truth when she heard it, even from herself. She straightened up abruptly. "Thanks for getting me this far. I think I can take it from here."

"You sure?" Jason's eyes wandered to two girls in bikini tops and mini-skirts who were coming toward them.

"Yeah. I'm sure."

Jason looked elated. "Well, I hope you feel better," he said as he backed down the street after the girls. "Maybe I'll see you later."

"Fat chance," Megan mumbled as she watched him turn and walk away. Megan hurried toward the service station.

A silver Honda Prelude was parked by the garage. Alyssa and Gabrielle were standing by it. With them was a petite woman dressed in a nurse's white uniform.

Much to Megan's dismay, all three had witnessed her incredible performance.

"What was *that* all about?" Gabrielle blurted out when Megan joined them.

Megan made a sour face. "Survival."

110

Gabrielle introduced Megan to her aunt. Kate Danzer looked more like Gabrielle's older sister than her aunt.

"Was that your boyfriend back there?" Kate asked Megan when they had gotten into her car.

"Him?" Megan snorted. "Hardly." She folded her arms across her chest and announced, "I just want you all to know that from this moment on, I'm through with boys."

"You?" Gabrielle turned around to look at Megan. "Never."

"I'm serious," Megan insisted. "You're looking at a changed girl. I intend to spend the rest of this spring break perfecting my tan and catching up on my reading. And that's it. Period."

"No boys?" Gabrielle repeated, as Kate pulled out of the station.

"None."

"No parties?"

"Absolutely not."

"No fun?"

"No way."

While Gabrielle and Megan bantered back and forth, Alyssa sat silently and thought about what had just happened at Dune Buggies. She was practically engaged to Brock Jorgensen, and yet she had thrown herself into the arms of another boy. And not just another boy, but a perfect stranger. And then she had let him kiss her.

But the very worst part of the whole thing was that she had enjoyed it. Maybe Megan was right. Maybe this spring break would change her life forever.

"Rise and shine!" Megan shouted as she strode through the guest room of Kate Danzer's condominium and threw open the curtains. "It's a glorious morning."

Gabrielle groaned and pulled her pillow over her head. "Nine more days of this?" she wailed. "I don't think I can take it."

Megan tugged at her arm. "Come on, Gabby, get up!"

"Why?" Gabrielle mumbled from beneath her pillow. "It's vacation, remember? We're *supposed* to sleep in."

"Are you out of your mind? We're in Coconut Beach! Fun, sun, and boys!"

Gabrielle sat up and blinked at the room around her. The matching twin bed had been freshly made. An overstuffed chair sat by the open French window, and a fresh breeze rustled the lace curtains. Gabrielle looked carefully at her friend. "I thought you were finished with boys."

"That was *college* boys." Megan put her hands on her hips and declared, "Today I am off in search of someone my own age."

Gabrielle fell back against her pillow. "Well, enjoy yourself."

"Oh, no, you don't!" Megan pulled Gabrielle back to a sitting position. "We've got a lot to do today. I promised Alyssa we'd help her shop for a bikini."

Gabrielle knew that any attempt to go back to sleep was a lost cause. She threw back the covers and sat on the edge of the twin bed. "Where's Aunt Kate?"

"At work," Megan replied. "She left a note on the fridge saying we should make ourselves at home. She made some orange juice for us before she left. Come have a glass and get dressed."

Gabrielle ran a hand through her dark hair. "Will I ever be able to call one day of this vacation my own?"

The phone rang. Megan ran from the room. "I'll get it," she called.

Alyssa, who had been asleep on the convertible sofa in the living room, stirred at the pounding of Megan's feet. She opened her eyes slowly. The blades of a white ceiling fan spun lazily from the wooden beam above her head. She blinked and turned her head. A lush, green fern hung above a glistening, white wicker armchair. It was a pretty room, like something from the pages of a magazine.

Alyssa had passed a restless night, full of strange, disquieting dreams. One now lingered in her memory. She had been on a silver beach, wearing a beautiful white dress, dancing with a boy she didn't know. The boy in her dream had had brown eyes and wavy brown hair. Suddenly, Alyssa sat bolt upright. Now she remembered. He was the boy she'd kissed at Dune Buggies.

"Alyssa!"

Alyssa looked around and saw Megan peeking out from the kitchen.

"Brock's on the phone," Megan whispered. "He wants to talk to you."

"How did he know I was here?" Alyssa asked as she lept out of bed.

"Maybe Shannon or Monica saw you with us last night."

Alyssa wondered what else Shannon or Monica might have seen. She hastily pulled a robe over her pink cotton nightgown and joined Megan in the kitchen.

"It's on the counter." Megan pointed to the telephone.

Alyssa perched on one of the high stools at the breakfast counter and picked up the receiver. "Hello?"

" 'Lyssa! Do you know what I had to go through to find you?" Brock sounded both concerned and angry.

Alyssa rubbed her forehead. "Well, now that you've found me," she said calmly, "what was it you wanted to tell me?"

Brock was silent for a moment. "I thought you'd be glad to hear from me."

"Not when you talk to me in that tone of voice. I'm not a child, Brock."

"Hold it, hold it," Brock said quickly. " 'Lyssa, I didn't mean to shout at you. I was just really worried."

"You didn't seem so worried when you left me stranded at Carter's Truck Stop yesterday."

Brock's voice tightened. "I asked you if you wanted a ride."

"No, you didn't. You announced you were leaving and that anyone who wanted to ride with you could come along."

"*You're* the one who yanked your bags out of my jeep," Brock retorted.

"Well, what else was I supposed to do? And I never expected you to just leave me like that. You knew my parents were away so they couldn't come get me. What did you expect me to do? Wait there overnight for the next bus back to Leesville?"

Brock sighed impatiently. "Come on, Alyssa. I knew you'd find a ride down here. Anyway, I don't know what you're so mad about. You started the whole thing by wanting to break up."

"No, I wanted to discuss our future," Alyssa replied firmly. "I got angry because you decided to go ahead and plan my whole life for me."

"All right, Alyssa. Look, maybe I was wrong. Maybe I should have talked to you first. But I want to talk to you now."

Alyssa sighed. "This isn't a very good time to talk."

"You're right, 'Lyssa," Brock said in his most soothing voice. "We shouldn't be talking about something so important over the phone. And things always come out wrong when you can't see the other person. Why don't I come over and—"

"No!" Alyssa cried. "Don't come over."

"Why?"

"I—I just need time—"

"Time for what?"

"To think about things," Alyssa stammered. "I mean, I'm not dressed, I haven't had a chance to—"

"I'll give you plenty of time to get dressed,"

Brock insisted. "I'm going to have breakfast with my grandparents first. I had to do some pretty fancy talking last night when I showed up without your you. But I handled it. They think you spent the night with some girlfriends planning the wedding. They're still a bit upset, so, like I said, I'm having breakfast with them and then I'll be right over."

"No, Brock, *don't*," Alyssa said firmly.

But Brock was adamant. "I'm coming over."

"You don't even know where Gabby's aunt lives," Alyssa protested desperately.

"I'll find the address in the phone book. Now Alyssa, just relax. I love you."

Alyssa stared at the receiver and listened to the dull hum of the dial tone. Slowly, she replaced the receiver in its cradle.

Megan came back into the kitchen and poured Alyssa a glass of fresh orange juice. "Is everything okay?"

"No, it's not, actually." Alyssa laughed bitterly. "Brock is the most pigheaded person I've ever met." She took the glass from Megan. "He's determined to come over here this morning."

Megan sat down on the stool next to Alyssa. "But don't you want to see him?"

"Not right now. I'm too confused—and too mad." Alyssa ruffled her hair in frustration.

"He's coming over right after he has breakfast with his grandparents."

"Just don't be here when he arrives." Gabrielle stood in the doorway to the kitchen and yawned. She was still in her nightshirt.

Alyssa set her glass down on the table. "*That* would show him. Brock thinks he can order me around. He always has."

Megan sprang off her stool. "Then what are we waiting for? I want everyone dressed and ready to go in ten minutes. We're going out to breakfast."

A half-hour later, the girls stood in front of Tugboat Tina's Saltwater Taffy and Marine Emporium. The shop was located in the old harbor area of Coconut Beach, an area brimming with countless little shops and restaurants. The storefronts were painted in blues and greens, faded by the salty gulf air.

Gabrielle held a paper cup of cappucino in one hand and a bag of saltwater taffy in the other. "I would never have thought of this combination in a thousand years."

Alyssa took a bite of saltwater taffy and rolled her eyes. "I think I've just died and gone to heaven," she said when she'd finished chewing.

Megan grinned. "Eating saltwater taffy for breakfast makes me feel deliciously wicked."

"Do you think it's fattening?" Alyssa asked as she bit into her fourth piece.

"Of course, it's fattening," Megan replied. "That's what makes it so deliciously wicked!"

The three girls wound their way down the street, stopping to browse in the window of each shop. When they reached a store called Animal Quackers, they decided to investigate.

"It's hard to believe so many stores in the same town, even on the same street, could all sell T-shirts and still make a profit," Gabrielle remarked. She held up a T-shirt decorated with a cartoon of elephants lounging on the beach. Its caption read, *Coconut Beach—Home of the Young and the Aimless.* "Who in their right mind would buy *this*? The rendering of the elephants is so amateurish."

Megan laughed. "The art critic has spoken."

Alyssa slipped on a pair of sunglasses decorated with huge, rhinestone studded flamingos. "I'd wear that T-shirt before I'd wear *these*."

Megan giggled. "Oh, Alyssa, they're you!"

Gabrielle perched a rainbow-striped beanie with a spinning propeller on top of her head. Alyssa draped a chain of little rubber sharks around her neck and the two girls stood in front of a floor-length mirror, striking funny poses.

"This is too good!" Megan reached in her bag for her camera. "I've got to get a shot of you guys. No one in Leesville will believe it." She held the camera up to her eyes. "Say, 'Surf's Up!' "

Gabrielle and Alyssa made big, toothy grins and chorused, "Surf's Up!"

Megan snapped the picture and forwarded the film. Alyssa lowered her sunglasses to the tip of her nose and peered archly over the top. "Okay," Megan said, as she raised the camera to her eye. "Say—" Megan lowered the camera. "Uh, oh."

"Uh, oh," both girls repeated, perfectly mimicking her startled inflection.

"No," Megan whispered. She pointed toward the door to the shop. "Look outside."

Alyssa turned and saw Brock just outside the picture window of the shop.

Gabrielle pulled Alyssa behind a large rack of postcards. "Do you want Brock to see you?" she whispered.

Alyssa shook her head. She definitely did not want to have another confrontation with Brock in public. And when she'd seen his face a moment ago, she couldn't help but notice its somber expression. Suddenly, the guilt she had felt about kissing the strange boy at Dune Buggies returned. How could she face Brock right now?

"What are you going to do?" Megan asked.

Alyssa removed the crazy sunglasses and twisted them in her hands. "Nothing."

Megan peeked out from behind the postcard rack and watched as Brock shoved his hands in his pockets and continued to stare forlornly at the display in the window.

"Look at him," Megan whispered. "He looks heartbroken."

"Megan!" Gabrielle scolded. "Don't be so melodramatic."

"I'm not. I'm just calling it like I see it." Megan sneaked to the front of the store to watch him more closely.

Megan's remark may have been melodramatic, but it wasn't far off the mark. Brock usually carried himself like a military officer, with his shoulders back, and his head held high. Now he stood with his shoulders slumped, and his head hanging, oblivious to the people passing by.

"He does look upset," Alyssa said feelingly. "Brock means well," she told Gabrielle. "It's just . . . I don't know. . . ."

Megan heard Alyssa's hesitation. "Go talk to him. Give him another chance. You owe him that."

"She doesn't *owe* him anything," Gabrielle insisted.

"Well, they've spent four years together," Megan retorted. "Doesn't that mean anything?"

"Of course, it does," Gabrielle agreed. "But Alyssa shouldn't be bullied into talking to him."

"I'm just not ready," Alyssa said quietly, almost to herself.

Megan and Gabrielle didn't hear her. They stood practically nose-to-nose, their voices growing louder with every word.

"All I'm saying," Megan argued, "is that two people who've meant so much to each other and who were planning to get married, shouldn't fall apart over one fight."

"What makes you such an expert on relationships?" Gabrielle demanded.

"I watch a lot of talk shows," Megan snapped.

"That figures," Gabrielle retorted. "Look, when Alyssa's ready to talk, she'll talk."

"And I'm not ready," Alyssa repeated, more loudly this time. "I'm not ready to talk. I'm not ready to get married. I am *just not ready!*"

Her outburst caught both Megan and Gabrielle by surprise. They looked at her in embarrassed silence.

"Anyway, Brock has gone."

Gabrielle and Megan spun around. Alyssa was right.

"If you two still want to bicker, you can do it

by yourselves," Alyssa said pleasantly. "I'm going shopping."

Gabrielle and Megan silently followed Alyssa out into the sunlight.

The girls continued to stroll up and down the heart of the old town, stopping occasionally in boutiques and souvenir shops. Gabrielle bought her father a visor with a tiny stuffed alligator on the brim. She planned to make him wear it as penance for having forced her to come to Florida. Megan's arms were laden down with bags full of T-shirts for her family and herself. Alyssa's one bag held a special, daring purchase, an electric-blue bikini Megan had practically browbeaten her into buying.

Finally, the three girls decided to stop for a cool drink at the Paradise Café. The patio was decorated with little, white wrought-iron tables shaded by colorful red-and-green striped umbrellas. Megan led the girls to an empty table overlooking the beach. She dropped her packages on the ground by her chair and sank into it with relief.

"Whew! My arms were about to fall off."

"My feet were about to fall off," Gabrielle said as she slipped into her chair. "But are you really thinking about food when we just ate an entire pound of saltwater taffy?"

"I'm not thinking of food," Megan replied. "I'm thinking of sightseeing."

"Sitting down?" Alyssa asked as she slid into the middle chair.

"Um-hmm." Megan pointed to several muscular guys who were playing volleyball on the beach. "Now, that's what I call great scenery."

Gabrielle shook her head and laughed. "Megan, you are incredible."

"Thank you."

"I didn't mean it as a compliment."

"That's okay." Megan watched a boy carrying a surfboard. "I took it as one."

"Is that really all you think about?" Alyssa asked. "Boys?"

"Of course not," Megan replied. "I think about lots of other things. My parents, college, what I'm going to do with my life. But none of those things are fun to think about." She motioned for the waiter to take their order. "And because I'm on vacation, I'm out to have fun."

"What can I get for you?" the waiter asked when he came over.

Megan answered matter-of-factly. "A date."

The waiter's eyes twinkled with amusement. "I believe that can be arranged."

"And one for her, too." Megan gestured toward Gabrielle.

"I don't believe you," Gabrielle groaned.

Alyssa paid no attention to her friends' joking. She stared out at the crowded beach before her. Brock was out there, somewhere in Coconut Beach, and sooner or later she would have to talk to him.

"Maybe I'd better change our order," Megan said, as she grinned at the waiter. "Just bring us three root beers, with lots of ice."

The waiter bowed. "Coming right up."

"Why do you insist on embarrassing me?" Gabrielle asked when the waiter had gone.

"I was just kidding around," Megan said. "He knew that. Come on, Gabby, lighten up."

"I will. But don't push." Gabrielle turned to Alyssa. "Megan is the pushiest person I know."

Alyssa shook her small, pink cellophane shopping bag. "I agree completely. I never would have bought this bikini on my own."

Megan pretended to pout. "You don't *really* think I'm pushy, do you?"

Gabrielle and Alyssa replied in unison. "Yes."

"Well, being pushy is a good way to meet boys," Megan said. "You can't tell me you don't want to meet boys."

"Of course I want to meet boys," Gabrielle replied. "But in my own way and in my own time. I don't like to throw myself at the first male that passes by *just* because he's male."

"I don't throw myself at boys," Megan protested. "I just flirt."

"Call it what you will," Gabrielle said with a shrug. "But yesterday in Chad's car, I watched you heave yourself at Jason in a major way. And something weird was going on between you two last night. You never did tell us what happened, and why you were hobbling along."

Megan had been trying to block the entire Jason episode out of her mind. "Okay, maybe I was a *little* overeager," she admitted, "but I've learned my lesson."

The waiter brought their sodas, and as he set Megan's on the table, he winked. As if to prove she *had* learned her lesson, Megan folded her hands demurely on the table in front of her and said politely, "Thank you very much."

The waiter raised his eyebrows, surprised the game had ended so abruptly. "You're welcome," he said and walked away.

Megan took a long sip of her soda and set it back on the table. "If you *were* going to throw yourself at someone, Gabby, who would it be?" She pointed to a heavily muscled boy playing volleyball. "Someone like him?"

Gabrielle watched as the boy spiked the volleyball over the net, then turned and gave one of his teammates a high five. "No, I think he's more Alyssa's type."

"What's my type?" Alyssa asked absently.

"You know," Megan said, "guys who work out, like Brock."

"Brock's definitely muscular," Alyssa said, "but I don't know if he's my *type*."

"What?" Megan sputtered. "You've been going with him for four years. How can he *not* be your type?"

"What I mean is, if Brock and I break up, I don't know if I'd be attracted to someone muscular or not. Frankly, I'm so confused right now," Alyssa said as she poked her ice cubes with her straw. "I don't know if I *have* a type."

Megan turned back to Gabrielle. "How about those guys?" She pointed to a group of boys at another table. They were building an elaborate pyramid out of their plastic cups. Their plain, white T-shirts covered their already peeling sunburns.

Gabrielle smiled. "They're a little on the nerdy side. They remind me of Heath Perkins."

Megan threw her hands in the air and leaned back in her seat. "Then I give up," she declared.

"Actually, I like someone sort of in between the jock and the nerd."

Gabrielle glanced around the patio and her eyes came to rest on a boy sitting alone at a table in the far corner. His hair was light brown, streaked with gold from the sun, and he wore a pair of horn-rimmed glasses. A book lay open on the table and he paused between bites of a hamburger to turn the page. Gabrielle smiled and said, "Someone like him."

Megan gave her a playful little shove. "Why don't you go talk to him?"

Gabrielle stiffened. "Are you kidding? He's reading. And besides, I'd never do anything like that."

"Then how are you going to meet him?"

"I didn't say I wanted to *meet* him," Gabrielle said. "I just meant that he seemed more my type, that's all."

"Go on." Megan shoved her a little harder. "I dare you to talk to him."

Gabrielle recognized the taunting look in Megan's eyes. She remembered it from when they were children. It was usually followed by Megan calling her a chicken, or a scaredy-cat. The look had always made her furious. Gabrielle stared hard at Megan. Then she shoved her chair back and stood up.

"All right. I will."

"What?" Megan's mouth dropped open.

"You're kidding, aren't you?" Alyssa asked.

Gabrielle didn't reply. She had no intention of actually talking to the boy, but she'd make Megan think she had. She'd pause by the boy's table for a moment, just long enough for him to look up at her. Then she'd move along and make her way back to her table.

Just before she reached the boy's table, Gabrielle glanced over her shoulder to make sure Megan and Alyssa were watching her. When she turned back, her foot caught on a leg of the table and she tripped. Her glass tipped in her hand and soda spilled out onto his open book.

"Oh, no!" Gabrielle put her hand down in front of the rushing liquid in a futile attempt at keeping it from dripping into his lap. "I'm so sorry!"

The boy stood quickly and knocked over his chair in the process. He snatched up his book and shook it out over the patio floor. "That's all right," he said.

"No, it's not all right." Gabrielle grabbed a few paper napkins from the dispenser on his table and dabbed at the damp pages. "Your book. I've ruined it."

"It's not ruined," he insisted, as he took one of the napkins from her and pressed it against the cover. "It's just a little soggy."

Gabrielle read the title aloud, *"Siddhartha*. I love that book!"

The boy looked at her for the first time and smiled. "You've read it?" Gabrielle noticed he was very handsome up close. His pale, green eyes stood out dramatically from his deeply tanned face. "It's my second time through."

Gabrielle smiled and looked again at the book. "I'm so sorry I ruined the cover for you."

The boy laughed a bit embarrassedly. "Well, you know what they say. It's not the cover that's important. It's what's inside."

Gabrielle laughed with him. "Yes, well . . ." Suddenly she felt a little wobbly in the knees. She knew if she stayed one second longer, she might do something even more embarrassing, like knock over his entire table. "I've got to go now," she said quickly.

The boy smiled. "Maybe I'll see you around the beach."

"Maybe."

Gabrielle walked back to her table wearing a silly grin. The little adventure had really lifted her spirits. She had met someone in her own way, if not exactly in her own good time.

Megan had admiration written all over her face. "Smooooooooth move! I *never* would have thought of that myself."

"Me, either," Alyssa agreed. "I'd have been too scared."

Gabrielle realized that Megan and Alyssa thought she had spilled her drink on purpose, and she wasn't about to correct them. She sat down in her chair. "Thanks. It was just a burst of inspiration."

"You're finally getting into the vacation spirit," Megan declared, "and that deserves a toast." She raised her glass in the air. "To inspiration!"

"Don't look now," Megan whispered when she'd swallowed, "but *my* type has just arrived." Alyssa and Gabrielle each started to turn around and Megan hissed, "I said, don't look!"

The girls turned back and waited for Megan to give them permission to move. She crossed her legs, rested her chin on her hand, and looked dreamily in the boy's direction. "He's tall," she said, barely moving her lips. "Maybe about six foot-three. And slim. He's got beautiful brown hair, kind of wavy, and a great tan. He's got to be some sort of athlete; I can tell from the way he walks. And something about him looks vaguely familiar."

"Familiar? Gabrielle asked. "Megan, this is getting ridiculous. When can we turn around?"

"Wait until he sits down," Megan replied. She tossed her blond hair off of her shoulder in what she hoped was her most seductive manner. Suddenly, she stiffened. "Oh, my God! You won't believe this, but he's coming this way." Her eyes grew wider. "I mean, he's heading *directly* for our table!"

The boy came up to the table and stopped. Megan looked up at him with a beautiful smile. She was about to say hello when the boy spoke first.

"Alyssa?"

Alyssa looked at him. A pair of unforgettable brown eyes met hers, and her hand flew to her mouth. "It's you!"

"The boy from Carter's Truck Stop," Megan cried.

Alyssa smiled nervously. "Yes, this is the boy who helped me when I was getting my bags . . ." Alyssa stopped and blushed.

"We haven't been formally introduced," the boy said. "You left in such a hurry last night."

"You met again at Dune Buggies?" Megan exclaimed. "Where was I?"

"Somewhere with Jason," Gabrielle replied.

The boy smiled at the three girls and put out his hand for Alyssa to shake. "I'm Dylan McLean."

"Pleased to meet you," Alyssa replied properly. "And these are my friends, Megan Becker and Gabrielle Danzer."

Dylan shook each girl's hand in turn. "Pleased to meet you."

135

Megan caught Gabrielle's eye and attempted to mouth a message. *"Now* I understand why Alyssa wasn't ready to see you-know-who."

"Pardon?" Dylan cocked his head in her direction.

"I was just saying that it's quite a coincidence that you two met at Carter's, then last night at Dune Buggies, and now, here you are again!"

Dylan laughed. "Well, Coconut Beach isn't all that big. Sooner or later you run into everyone."

His words rang like a warning bell in Alyssa's ears and she glanced nervously over her shoulder for any sign of Brock.

Gabrielle sensed Alyssa's discomfort. "You know, I've noticed the beach is less crowded to the north."

"Really?" Alyssa asked brightly.

"Not today," Dylan said. "A big windsurfing competition's been going on since early this morning."

"I've always wanted to watch windsurfing," Alyssa said. The moment the words were out of her mouth, she realized they sounded like an invitation for Dylan to take her to the competition.

Gabrielle realized the same thing. "Then why don't you go watch it?"

Megan sprang out of her chair. "Why don't we all go?"

Gabrielle looked meaningfully at Megan. "You and I have *other* plans, remember?"

Megan knit her brow. "What other plans?"

"We're having our hair done for the crab feast." Gabrielle raised her eyebrows for emphasis.

Megan nodded wisely. "Oh, *those* other plans." She looked over at Alyssa. "You two go ahead without us."

"What do you say, Alyssa?" Dylan asked.

"All right. That would be nice." Alyssa dug in her purse and placed a dollar on the table. "That's for my soda. I'll meet you back at Kate's this afternoon."

"I'll take your package back if you like. Have a good time."

Alyssa smiled gratefully. "Thanks, Gabby."

"Don't forget the crab feast tonight," Megan called as Alyssa and Dylan moved away from the table. "*Everyone* from Leesville will be there."

Alyssa knew Megan was reminding her that "everyone" included Brock Jorgensen. "Don't worry, Megan," Alyssa replied. "I'll be back in plenty of time."

Before they'd gone twenty feet along the beach, Dylan stopped. "I have a confession to make," he said.

"What?"

"Running into you just now wasn't exactly a coincidence."

"It wasn't?"

Dylan ran one hand through his wavy hair. "I must have walked up and down Main Street twenty times this morning. I was about to start number twenty-one when I spotted you and your friends in the Paradise Café."

The breeze off the water ruffled Alyssa's hair and sent a shiver of delight through her body. She wasn't brave enough to confess that she'd dreamed about him the night before, or that the image of his face had stayed with her all morning. Instead, she said, "I'm glad you found me."

"When you ran out of Dune Buggies last night, I felt a bit like the prince in Cinderella. Only you didn't leave a glass slipper. Just a first name."

"Sorry about that," Alyssa said with a self-conscious laugh. "Like I told you, I had a rough day."

"Well, you're in Coconut Beach now." With a broad wave of his arm, Dylan gestured to the glistening water spread out before them. "Where there's never a cloud in the sky, where happiness is the only emotion, and where the most unexpected things can happen." He paused and smiled. "If you let them."

"Did you ever think of working for the local tourist office?" Alyssa teased.

Dylan grinned. "I love this place. It's like a home away from home for me. I've been coming here for years."

By now, Alyssa and Dylan had reached the area of the beach sectioned off for the windsurfing contest. A large crowd had gathered to watch the flotilla of windsurfers on the gulf. Suddenly, a shrill whistle sounded from the judging platform erected on the shore.

"Is that the start of the race?" Alyssa asked.

"It's not so much a race as a contest of skills," Dylan said. "Each surfer has to execute certain moves in a limited amount of time. Then he's awarded points for how well he performs. The one with the most points wins." He shrugged. "Simple, right?"

"Outstanding move!" a boy in a blue tank top and baggy shorts cheered. Several other guys beside him cupped their hands around their mouths and chanted, "Aiken, Aiken, he's our man, if he can't do it, nobody can!"

"They're rooting for Jay Aiken," Dylan explained, pointing toward a lone figure out on the surf. "He's on the sailboard with the turquoise and fluorescent pink sail."

Alyssa put her hand to her eyes to shield them

from the sun and followed the direction of his hand. "Do you know him?"

Dylan nodded. "He's my good buddy. We drove down together from Ashton."

"Ashton? But that's only about ten miles from where I live. I'm from Leesville."

"You're from Leesville? I'll bet we know some of the same people."

"Probably." Alyssa racked her brain for a moment but her mind drew a complete blank. "This is silly," Alyssa said. "I *know* I know people from Ashton. But at the moment, I can't think of a single one."

Dylan shrugged good-naturedly. "That's all right. You've got the rest of the week to remember."

The impossible idea of spending nine days with Dylan made Alyssa's insides flutter.

A loud cheer erupted from the crowd as Jay Aiken burst over the top of a huge wave in a one-footed jump.

"That looks dangerous," Alyssa said.

"It can be," Dylan said. "In the early morning contest Mike Collins got slammed pretty bad. He'd just done a downwind turn and was carving the wave when a monster gust of wind slammed him into his sail." Dylan shook his head. "He was lucky he wasn't killed. Those boards are going twenty-five, thirty miles an hour. It's like hitting a concrete wall."

Alyssa looked at the wetsuited boy on the pink-and-blue sailboard with new respect.

"Watch this," Dylan instructed. "Jay's getting ready to do his forward loop."

Alyssa watched as the boy swooped over the top of a big wave, dipped the nose of his board, and did a complete forward roll.

"All right, Aiken!" the boys next to her bellowed.

"He's only got his helicopter to do, and he's finished," Dylan explained.

"How do you know so much about windsurfing?" Alyssa asked.

Dylan grinned, once again revealing the dimple in his left cheek. "I dabble a little in the sport myself."

"Hey, Dylan," one of the boys nearby called. "Are you worried?"

Dylan tugged on his earlobe and laughed. "Maybe a little."

"What are they talking about?" Alyssa asked.

"Oh, I competed in the contest this morning," Dylan replied sheepishly. "I guess I did okay."

"Get out of town, McLean!" a tall, skinny guy cut in. He turned to Alyssa. "Dylan's the reigning board champ. He's been undefeated for over a year. But Aiken's gaining on him."

"You're dreaming!" the first boy hooted. "No one can catch the Wizard." He clapped Dylan on the back. "My money's on you, big guy."

Alyssa watched how Dylan handled his friends' praise and was impressed. It was obvious the attention embarrassed him, but he remained good-natured. Alyssa knew that if Brock were a windsurfing champion, he'd make sure everyone he met knew it.

A beach vendor in a red-and-white striped shirt rode by on a bicycle.

"Alyssa, why don't I buy you an ice cream to celebrate our new friendship?" Dylan asked.

Alyssa smiled. "An ice cream would be perfect." She knew he was using the appearance of the vendor as an opportunity to change the subject.

"I'm starved," Dylan said. "I didn't eat breakfast. I can never eat right before a contest. And all I ate on the way down yesterday were some potato chips, three peanut butter-and-jelly sandwiches, and a gallon of soda."

"That's *all*?"

Dylan snapped his fingers. "Oh, yeah, when we stopped at Carter's, I had a chili burger and onion rings."

Alyssa laughed at the hungry expression on Dylan's face.

"Don't go away. I'll be right back." Dylan ran after the beach vendor.

Alyssa turned back to watch the windsurfers. A moment later, she felt a hand on her arm. She smiled and turned. "Are they out of—Brock!"

Brock stood beside her, his expression grim.

"Wha-what are you . . . How long have you been standing there?" Alyssa wondered if Brock had seen her talking with Dylan, and the guilt she felt earlier returned.

"I went by Gabrielle's aunt's condo, but you'd already gone," Brock said scoldingly.

"I told you not to come over," Alyssa said with a quick glance around the beach.

"Aw, come on, 'Lyssa." Brock's voice was low and intimate and he took a small step closer. "Don't be angry. I'm sorry I left you at Carter's. I'll never do anything like that again, okay?"

Alyssa felt her throat tighten with panic. This was no time for Brock to work his familiar magic on her, not when Dylan would be rejoining her in a minute or two. She was in a terribly awkward position, and although Alyssa had been well trained to gracefully handle all sorts of social situations, this particular one had never come up. "Okay," Alyssa replied distractedly.

Brock kissed her sweetly on the cheek. "Then I'm forgiven?"

Alyssa heard herself say, in an overly cheerful voice, "Of course you are!"

Brock nodded with satisfaction. "Good." He looked around, as if seeing the crowd around them for the first time. "What are you doing here, anyway?"

"I was watching the windsurfing contest," Alyssa replied honestly. For a brief moment she wondered if feigning illness would be too dramatic a way out of this embarrassing situation. She smiled in spite of her awkwardness. That would be something Megan Becker would do.

"I didn't know you knew anything about windsurfing," Brock said.

"I don't." Alyssa racked her brain. Why couldn't she think of a way to prevent Brock from meeting Dylan? But it was too late. Dylan had come up behind Brock, an ice cream bar in each hand.

"Dylan was explaining the rules to me," Alyssa said, gesturing nervously to the other boy.

"Dylan?" Brock's eyebrows knit together in a frown as he turned around.

"Dylan McLean." The boy stepped past Brock and handed one of the ice cream bars to

Alyssa. He then put out his free hand to shake Brock's.

"Dylan," Alyssa said smoothly. "I'd like you to meet Brock Jorgensen, a . . . a friend of mine from Leesville."

Brock shot her a questioning glance. "How do you do," he said stiffly.

"I've seen you play," Dylan said. "Even though I always have to root against your team."

"Dylan is from Ashton," Alyssa explained. She kept a safe distance from Brock so he wouldn't be able to drape his arm around her shoulder the way he usually did. "I tried to think of the people I know from Ashton, but I drew a blank."

"How could you have drawn a blank?" Brock responded, eyeing her warily. "My cousins, the Eastmans, live in Ashton. Then there's Peter Orbison, Gayle Bellows—"

"Oh, that's right!" Alyssa interrupted with a forced giggle. "I must be losing my mind." She took a deep breath. "Well . . ."

Both boys smiled pleasantly and nodded, each expecting the other to leave.

Alyssa could think of no reasonable way out of the situation. A lie would have to do. She clapped her hand to her forehead. "Oh, my gosh! I just remembered I promised to meet Megan and Gabrielle back at Kate's for lunch. I've got to go."

"But—" both boys said at once.

"It was good seeing you," Alyssa said politely to Brock. "And it was nice meeting you," she nodded toward Dylan.

Brock and Dylan stared at Alyssa, each with a completely befuddled expression on his face. If the situation hadn't been so awful, Alyssa would have burst out laughing. And in her terrible nervousness, she did something worse than laugh. "I'll be going to the crab feast tonight on Porter's Island. See you there!"

Both boys raised a hand and called, "Right!"

"What have I done?" Alyssa let out a groan as she ran toward the road. "Now they'll *both* be at the party."

"I hope Alyssa knows what she's doing," Megan said, as she slipped into a short, silk skirt decorated with bright turquoise, orange, and green flowers.

She and Gabrielle were getting dressed for the crab feast. Megan's bed was covered with outfits she had tried on and rejected.

"I mean, what's Brock going to think when he finds out she spent part of the afternoon on the beach with another guy?" Megan pulled on a green off-the-shoulder peasant blouse and tucked it into her skirt. "Particularly a guy from Ashton."

When Alyssa had met Gabrielle and Megan at the condo earlier that afternoon, she had told them only the bare, neutral facts of her time with Dylan, omitting any mention of having met Brock. And then she'd changed her clothes and left the condo. She told Gabrielle and Megan she needed some time alone before the crab feast and she promised to see them at Porter's Island.

"Why should Alyssa care what Brock thinks?" Gabrielle stood in front of the mirror, brushing her hair. "Brock's the one who abandoned her, remember?"

"Come on, Gabby, they're the premier couple of Leesville High. They can't break up. Everyone is counting on them."

Gabrielle stopped brushing her hair and looked at Megan. "Why would Brock and Alyssa's staying together have anything to do with anybody else?"

"Haven't you ever noticed that break-ups are catching? If *they* split up, every other couple will follow their example."

Gabrielle rolled her eyes. "That's ridiculous."

"Well, you just watch and see."

Megan took her perfume and squirted it first on her wrist, then behind both ears, and finally behind each knee.

Gabrielle coughed and waved her hand in front of her face. "What are you trying to do, gag me to death?"

"I don't want my perfume to wear off in the damp sea air," Megan explained.

"You'd be better off if it *does*," Gabrielle said,

wrinkling up her nose. "That stuff smells like bug spray."

"Really?" Megan fanned her face with her hand. "Maybe I should wash some off. Guys hate too much perfume."

"If you overwhelm them with your charming personality," Gabrielle teased, "they won't notice the perfume."

"Very funny." Megan began to apply an extra coat of mascara to her eyelashes. "Have you decided what you're going to wear tonight, Gabby?"

Gabrielle looked down at her black shorts and black jersey. "This."

Megan froze with her mascara wand in midair. "Are you sure?"

"Of course I'm sure." Gabrielle cocked her head defensively. "What's wrong with it?"

"Well, it's just so, so *black*." Megan recapped the mascara and explained. "You need color to brighten your looks."

"But I like black," Gabrielle said, tucking her hair behind her ears. "It's dramatic."

"It's dreary," Megan said bluntly. "Look." She pointed at Gabby's open suitcase on the bed. "Nothing in there has any pizzazz."

"For your information, most fashion experts consider black a classic," Gabrielle replied, snapping the suitcase shut with a loud click.

"Fine." Megan shrugged. "If you want to show up at the crab feast looking like you're in mourning, that's your problem."

"Oh, come on, Megan," Gabrielle sighed. "Who really cares what I look like?"

"Everyone cares, believe me." Megan rifled through the discarded clothes on her bed. She picked up a white mini-skirt that laced up the front, and an electric-pink knit top. "Here's just the thing."

"I can't wear that!" Gabrielle gasped. "It's not me."

"I'm going to create a new you." Megan took Gabrielle by the wrist and led her over to the dressing table. She shoved her onto the stool and pushed her black hair off her forehead. "Trust me. You're going to be beautiful."

Gabrielle pushed Megan's hand away in irritation. "Why is how I look so important to you?" she demanded.

Megan stepped back and put her hands on her hips. "Because tonight is the big party. Everyone from Leesville will be there. Shannon bought a brand new outfit just for this occasion."

"So?"

"So we have to look good, too."

"What do you mean, *we*?" Gabrielle turned to face Megan. "Are you afraid I'm going to embarrass you?"

Megan nibbled on the wooden tip of her make-up brush.

"That's it, isn't it?" Gabrielle cried.

"Okay, I'll admit it," Megan said. "Look, you wander around school dressed like the Black Widow, and people make fun of you behind your back."

"Do you think I care what Shannon Dobbler and her crew of clones say about me? I like the way I look. I like my style. That's all that matters." Gabrielle stood up and faced Megan. "You used to be a real individual, too. What happened? Now whatever Shannon Dobbler does, you do. And whatever she says, you agree with."

"That's not true!" Megan protested.

"Yes, it is," Gabrielle insisted. "You wanted to be a cheerleader so badly that you sold out."

"Just because I hang with the popular crowd, and have lots of friends doesn't mean I *sold out*."

"Some friends!" Gabrielle shot back. "They wouldn't even let you sit at their table at Carter's Truck Stop!"

Megan winced. "Well, that's just because their feelings were hurt," she replied, picking up a hair brush and jerking it roughly through her hair. "I was supposed to be riding down with *them* and staying at the Flamingo. They probably thought I abandoned them when I decided to stay with you."

"I can't imagine the feelings of the entire squad would be hurt over such a silly thing."

Megan pursed her lips. "I think you're just jealous."

"Jealous? Me?" Gabrielle put her hand to her chest.

"Yes. We used to be really good friends until I became a cheerleader. Then all of a sudden, you barely spoke to me anymore."

"You're the one who started to ignore *me,"* Gabrielle parried. "You were always too busy going to practice. And to slumber parties at Shannon's, and to swimming parties at Monica Levitt's," Gabrielle said. "Admit it. You cut me out of your life."

"Only because you wanted to be cut out," Megan retorted. "You wouldn't accept any of my new friends. In the beginning I tried to include you. . . ."

"Yeah, you'd invite me along, then Shannon and the others would ignore me. You never stuck up for me. Not once."

"They didn't *ignore* you. It's just that, well, they didn't know what to say to you. I mean, you don't like to do the same things they, I mean *we*, do."

"Look, Megan," Gabrielle said. "Why don't you go to the crab feast without me? We're not friends anymore, and that's just the way it is. It's nobody's fault."

"Okay, I will." Megan slammed her hair brush on the dressing table. "You can just stay here by yourself. See if I care." Megan turned and stormed out of the room. A moment later, the front door slammed and the apartment grew still.

Gabrielle stared at her reflection in the mirror for a long time. She pulled her hair off her face and turned her head from side to side. She looked at each of her features as if she had never seen them before. Finally, she let her hair fall back around her face and sighed.

Alyssa stood in the shadows of Ray's Boathouse and watched a big crowd of kids on the pier prepare to leave for the first crab feast of the season on Porter's Island. Alyssa made an attempt to join the group from Leesville several times, but couldn't.

Boats of all sizes and shapes were lined up along the dock like mismatched taxis, waiting to ferry people across the narrow strait. The lead boat was an old tub painted white and red. Several large, metal pots were lashed to either side of the deck house. The pots were intended to boil the crabs over open fires on the beach. Alyssa could see Mike Bibbit and Tom Hooper already on board, along with several boys who weren't from Leesville. They struck her as vaguely familiar and then she recognized them as Dylan's friends from the windsurfing competition. Alyssa clenched her hands together. As far as she could tell, Dylan wasn't on the boat and neither was Brock.

A sleek racer was moored right behind the lead boat. Shannon Dobbler was seated next to the driver. Monica Levitts and a few of the other girls from the squad sat behind Shannon, chatting while they waited for the boats to leave the pier.

Alyssa's attention was caught by the sudden appearance of Megan Becker running down the dock. She passed Alyssa without seeing her. "Wait for me!"

"Becker the Wrecker is here!" Tom Hooper shouted from the lead boat. Megan put her hands on her hips and stuck her tongue out at him. "I wish people would give me a break, and quit calling me that," Megan shouted back. "I have a couple of car accidents—"

"Oh, all right. Come on, Megan," Tom called. "Hurry up and get on. It wouldn't be a party without you."

As Megan was about to board the lead boat, Shannon Dobbler called out cattily. "Where's your friend?" She snapped her fingers several times. "What's her name?"

"Shannon, you've made your point," Megan retorted. "You don't like Gabrielle, and you're mad at me. I know it, and everyone else knows it, so lay off."

Shannon was taken aback. Megan usually never talked to her with anything but deference. "Boy, are we touchy tonight."

Alyssa watched as the lead boat moved slowly away from the dock. Shannon's boat followed. One by one, the other boats followed in a watery parade toward Porter's Island. Their running lights made a twinkling necklace over the water. Across the strait, Alyssa could make out the blaze of a bonfire on the shore lighting up the evening sky. The sound of laughter and chatter from the open boats soon faded to silence.

The quiet descended upon Alyssa like a blanket. She leaned against a piling and rubbed her aching temples. After leaving Brock and Dylan on the beach, and after a brief stop at Kate's to let Gabrielle and Megan know her plans, she had walked aimlessly for hours, trying to make sense of the conflicting feelings churning inside her. Finally, Alyssa had come to a decision, the one she hoped was the best for everyone involved. But instead of relief at having made up her mind about what to do, Alyssa only felt tired.

A movement on the dock caught her eye and Alyssa watched a familiar figure in white shorts and a green-striped rugby shirt climb out of a silver-and-black speedboat and onto the wooden pier. He stared down the length of the pier toward the road, then ran his hand through his wavy brown hair. He seemed to be waiting for someone.

Alyssa checked her reflection in the darkened window of the boathouse.

"Dylan?" Alyssa stepped out of the shadows.

Dylan's face lit up in a smile of welcome. "Hi. I was hoping you'd come. I thought at first that I'd missed you."

He held out his hand to help her board the boat but Alyssa remained where she was standing. Her heart was pounding.

"I have a confession to make," Alyssa said softly.

"What is it?"

"Brock and I are engaged. To be married."

Dylan smiled sadly. "I know."

"How could you?" Of all the things Alyssa had expected him to say, "I know" was not one of them.

Dylan jammed his hands in his pockets and turned to look out over the water. "After you left the beach this morning, Brock and I had a long talk."

"I see. Did he tell you about me, about our fight?"

Dylan shook his head. "He didn't tell me about a fight." He smiled wryly. "But it didn't take me long to get the picture. First, though, Brock talked about football. You know, his scholarship, how he thought he'd do this year as a freshman starter, his plans to be a coach someday."

Alyssa smiled. "That sounds like Brock."

"And then he said you two were planning to get married, but that you hadn't really agreed on a date yet."

"That's the understatement of the year," Alyssa said with a little laugh. "We had a huge fight about it on our drive down here." She looked closely at Dylan's face. "When I first saw you at Carter's, Brock was on his way to Coconut Beach without me."

"Not a smart move."

Alyssa stared down at her hands clasped tightly in front of her, and whispered, "No, it wasn't."

Dylan looked away abruptly, and they stood side by side in silence.

"Look," Dylan said after a moment, "I'm shirking my duty as captain of this vessel." He was trying hard to keep the tone of his voice light. "I'm supposed to be ferrying people over to the island."

Alyssa glanced over her shoulder. "I was hoping to catch Brock before he went to the party. We have some things we need to talk over."

"He may already be there," Dylan replied.

"I don't think so. I didn't see him get on any of the boats."

"If he's not at the party," Dylan said as he caught the edge of the boat with his foot and pulled it toward the pier, "I'll bring you back. It'll only take ten minutes."

"It's a deal."

Dylan hopped in the boat and offered her his hand. She took it and stepped aboard.

"Is this your boat?" Alyssa asked as she settled into the seat beside him.

"No," Dylan replied. He untied the rope from its mooring on the pier. "It belongs to Jay Aiken's dad. Mr. Aiken has a summer place down here and he keeps the Bayliner for us to use."

Dylan started the outboard motor, and the engine roared to life. He shoved them off from the pier with a push of his arm. Once they were in deeper water, he eased the throttle forward and they moved quickly away from the shore in a wide arc. When Dylan increased the speed, the front of the boat lifted above the water and Alyssa had the sensation of flying across its surface.

Dylan turned to look at her. "So it's really going to happen," he shouted over the noise of the engine.

Alyssa nodded firmly. "It's what everyone wants."

"Everyone?"

"My mother and father couldn't be more thrilled about having Brock as a son-in-law. His family's one of the oldest and finest in Leesville.

And his parents are just as enthusiastic about it. And so are his grandparents."

"What about you?" Dylan asked.

"What do you mean?"

"Is it what *you* really want?"

"Well. . . ." She twisted the promise ring on her finger as she searched for the right words. She had made her decision and she would stick to it. "I've been pretty hesitant lately. Brock insists it's just cold feet."

"What are you hesitant about?"

"Well, marriage is a lifetime commitment," Alyssa replied. "Or it should be. We're very young to be making such a big decision. And Brock and I have, well, differences."

"Different opinions?"

Alyssa shook her head. "More like different ways of looking at things. Sometimes I worry our life views will just get more different over the years, and eventually pull us apart."

"That's a legitimate fear."

"Do you really think so?"

"Sure. Right now, you've still got a lot in common. The same school, the same friends, the same town. But what happens when the two of you move away? Or when you get involved in something in college that Brock can't be a part of? It's natural that over time a lot of the externals will change. The two of you will have to be able to agree on the basics."

"Oh, we do," Alyssa said quickly. "I mean, eventually I *do* want to get married, and have children. But—"

"But what?"

"Lately I've had the feeling that if I get married now, I'll never be able to do the things I've always dreamed of," Alyssa said earnestly. "And I wonder if in ten years I'll feel I've missed something. See, I've been with Brock since the ninth grade. I never dated anyone else, ever. And I've never really been on my own."

Alyssa smiled at Dylan. "Do you want to know my secret wish?"

"What?"

"I'd like to postpone college for a year or two and travel to Europe."

"Really?"

Alyssa nodded. "There're so many wonderful places I've only seen in pictures. I'd like to pick wildflowers in the Alps, or take a boat down the Rhine, or sit in a café in Paris."

"Then do it."

"Oh, I couldn't!" Alyssa laughed sadly. "My parents would kill me. They've got every detail of my next four years at college all worked out, even down to where Brock and I are going to live—married student housing."

161

"Sounds grim." Dylan chuckled. "I don't mean to pry, but have you ever talked to Brock about your dream?"

Alyssa shook her head. "Not really. Every time I bring it up, he tells me I'm being silly. Then he hugs me and I let it drop." Alyssa leaned back in her seat. "I was hoping to talk about a lot of things with Brock during this spring break, but we got off on the wrong foot."

Dylan cleared his throat. "You know, Alyssa, I bet that if you told Brock how you really feel, he'd understand. I don't think he'd pressure you into getting married right away. Maybe he'd even encourage you to take that trip to Europe."

"I don't think he'd go that far!"

"He might surprise you. I only talked to Brock for a little while, but he seemed like a decent guy. If he really—" Dylan cleared his throat again and continued. "If he really loves you, he'd want you to be happy."

"I should give him the benefit of the doubt. It's just that in our relationship everything has always been Brock's way. I'm not used to having people listen to me."

Dylan winked. "Hey, maybe Brock will decide to go to Europe *with* you."

Alyssa threw back her head and laughed.

"Brock would never go to a country where English wasn't the official language. I don't mean to put him down. That's just the way he is."

Alyssa was silent for a moment. When she spoke, her voice was so low that Dylan had to strain to hear her. "I can't believe I'm telling you all these personal things. I've never talked like this to a boy."

"That's because anything you say is safe with me," Dylan replied softly. "In a few minutes you'll be reunited with the guy who's going to marry you, and I'll be out of your life forever."

They both stared ahead at the glowing bonfires on the shore of Porter's Island. After a moment, Dylan said quietly, "Look, I may be way out of line, but . . ."

He flipped open the boat's storage compartment and, taking out a pen, scrawled something on a scrap of paper.

"If things don't work out between you and Brock, or if you ever just want to get together for a soda, or to talk—" He thrust the paper into her hand. "Here's my number."

Alyssa stared down at the paper.

"You can throw it away the minute I drop you off," Dylan said. "I'd understand if you did."

Before Alyssa could answer, the boat's engine coughed, sputtered, and abruptly died. Dylan

163

turned the key in the ignition but nothing happened. The boat drifted forward in the bay.

Dylan began to check the gauges. "We seem to be having a little engine trouble."

Alyssa looked back across the water at the island. They were so close she could see the figures of people on the shore. "And we were almost there."

"Yeah." Dylan went to the rear of the boat and knelt down by the outboard motor. He snapped open a canvas cover, exposing a red metal fuel tank resting in the small alcove. "Don't worry, we can always swim the rest of the way."

"Swim?" Alyssa looked down at the dark and forbidding water and shivered.

"I was just kidding." Dylan chuckled. And then the smile vanished from his face. "I've found the problem."

"What is it?" Alyssa asked.

"Oh, brother." Dylan stood up and rubbed his hand along the back of his neck. "I know this looks like a set-up, like I got you out here. . . ."

"Dylan!" Alyssa cut in. "What's the matter?"

He looked at her sheepishly. "We're out of gas."

Gabrielle arrived on the pier only a few minutes after Alyssa and Dylan had left. A gray

164

cabin cruiser with blue trim was pulling away from the dock. Gabrielle spotted Brock and Nat Farrell by the bow and she shouted after them. "Wait! Wait for me!"

But no one heard her call. And by the time she reached the end of the dock, the boat was a good way out on the water.

"Oh, terrific," Gabrielle mumbled. "Now I'm all dressed up with no place to go."

Though Gabrielle was still wearing the black shorts and jersey, she had added a pair of Megan's hot-pink earrings to her outfit. She hoped Megan would understand the gesture as one of peace. After Megan had stormed out of the apartment, Gabrielle had thought a lot about what had really happened between them in the past few years. Megan was partly right. Gabrielle had never made an effort to get to know Megan's new friends; she had been jealous of them from the start. Megan had found Shannon's friendship more interesting than hers, and it had hurt. Well, it was time to grow up. Megan had a right to live her own life.

"Excuse me. Are you lost?"

Gabrielle turned to see a boy in faded jeans and a blue sweatshirt sitting in a twin-hulled speedboat.

"Not exactly," Gabrielle replied. "Stranded is

more like it." She pointed toward the light of the bonfires in the distance. "I was trying to get to the crab feast on Porter's Island."

"Oh," the boy said as he stowed a tackle box and a small cooler beneath the seat. "I just watched about ten boatloads of people cruise out there."

"Do you think anyone'll be coming back?"

"Probably not until they're scheduled to, about three hours from now. Of course, if they knew they'd left you stranded here at the pier," the boy added with a grin, "they'd come back in no time."

Gabrielle smiled self-consciously. "I guess I'll just have to wait here," she said, "and hope for the best."

"Listen, I'm heading out to the reef to do a little night fishing. If you'd like, I'll give you a ride."

Gabrielle wondered if getting in a boat with a stranger was as bad as getting in a car with one. The crazy thought made her smile again.

"My name's Bradley Chase," the boy added, as if he'd read her thoughts. "I live here in Coconut Beach. My family owns that restaurant." He pointed toward a brightly lit building at the edge of the wharf. An elaborately carved wooden sign hung above the red door. The sign read, "The Sea Hawk—est. 1947."

It had taken all of Gabrielle's courage to follow Megan to the party, and she knew that if she hesitated any longer, she might lose her nerve and go home. "I'd love a ride," she declared.

"Great." The boy cleared his fishing gear off the metal seat in the bow of the boat. "Hop in."

As Gabrielle stepped on board, the boat rocked and several inches of water sloshed around her feet.

"We won't sink," Bradley reassured her. "It rained a few days ago and I haven't gotten around to bailing it out. Here." He pulled off his sweatshirt and laid it across the seat.

Bradley's boat was deceptively fast and skimmed across the water at a terrific clip. Within minutes, they were in sight of the cabin cruiser and closing fast. Gabrielle was surprised they had caught up so quickly until she realized the cruiser wasn't moving. Then she noticed another, smaller boat drifting alongside the larger vessel.

"Something's going on up ahead!" Gabrielle called to Bradley.

Bradley promptly cut the engine and they drifted closer.

Gabrielle saw Alyssa standing in the smaller boat, looking up at Brock, who was leaning over the rail of the cabin cruiser. Although they were still a few hundred yards away, their angry voices could be heard easily across the water.

"Looks like engine trouble," Bradley said.

Gabrielle winced. "It looks like more than that."

"**Y**ou ran out of *gas*?"

The sarcasm in Brock's voice was unmistakable. He gripped the rail of the cabin cruiser with both hands, as if it were the only thing preventing him from leaping into the smaller boat. "Do you really expect me to believe that?"

"Yes, I expect you to believe it," Alyssa replied indignantly. "How could you even think I would lie to you?"

"Check it yourself," Dylan said, gesturing toward the gas tank.

Brock ignored Dylan. "I'll tell you why I could think it," he said to Alyssa. "You told me you met this guy on the beach this morning. Well, I found out this afternoon you were with him last night."

"I wasn't *with* him last night," Alyssa protested.

"Are you telling me you didn't see him at Dune Buggies?" Brock asked.

Alyssa froze and wondered if someone had told Brock about the kiss. "Yes, I saw Dylan at Dune Buggies," she answered calmly, "just like I saw hundreds of other people."

"So you admit you were sneaking around on me."

"No! You're twisting my words again!" Alyssa shook her head in frustration. Brock always did this to her. "Look, Brock. Yesterday was just a bad day all around," she said. "I'd like to put it behind us and go forward."

"You can't brush this off," Brock continued. "First, you try to call off the wedding in front of my best friends. Then, you run out on me at Carter's. Next, you treat me like a casual acquaintance when we meet on the beach. And now you're going out with another guy. What am I supposed to think? The evidence is pretty clear."

"Stop talking like a lawyer, and talk to *me*, Brock!" Alyssa shouted. "I came looking for *you* tonight. Dylan just offered to take me to the island. Then we ran out of gas. That's all there is to it."

"She's right, Brock," Dylan said evenly. "Don't make matters worse."

"I'm not talking to you," Brock barked at Dylan.

"I can't believe this is happening!" Alyssa put her hands to her temples. "Okay, Brock. Believe what you want. But Dylan was only trying to help."

"I'll bet he was." Brock turned away from the rail and shouted to the captain of the cabin cruiser. "Let's get out of here."

"Oh, Brock, please don't just leave," Alyssa pleaded. "That's what started this whole mess."

Brock turned back slowly. "No, you've got it all wrong, Alyssa. *You* started this whole mess. *You* ruined everything. I was ready to get married, just like we'd planned, and *you* decided you didn't want to."

"Everything was so rushed," Alyssa said. "I just needed time to think."

"I don't need time to think," Brock said coldly. "I've made up my mind."

"Brock, please don't be this way." Alyssa looked up at him as if he were a stranger. "It upsets me."

"You *should* be upset," he said, and the hurt and anger were audible in his voice. "You broke my heart."

"Brock, listen to me."

Brock turned once more to the captain. "Let's get out of here!"

"Wait a minute, Brock," Nat said. "We can't leave them out here adrift. If they're really out of gas—"

"You know that's a lie," Brock said simply.

Megan had been playing volleyball with Shannon and the rest of the squad when the sound of angry voices interrupted them. For a moment everyone on the beach looked around in confusion, uncertain of where the argument was coming from. Then someone spotted the three boats adrift out on the bay, and soon a crowd had gathered by the water. Though no words could be made out, the group recognized Alyssa and Brock's voices.

"Poor Alyssa," Megan said. "She must feel terrible."

"She ought to feel stupid," Shannon replied. "How could anybody be so obvious and not expect to get caught?"

"Caught?" Megan interrupted. "Doing what?"

"Plenty, I'm sure." Shannon looked closely at her carefully manicured nails. "It's obvious Alyssa's been two-timing Brock."

"How can you say that!" Megan protested.

"I have my sources."

The girls were interrupted by a rumble as the

blue-and-gray cabin cruiser pulled away from the smaller boats.

"I wonder what happened," Tom Hooper said. "Brock's boat is turning back toward the pier."

The third boat, a slight aluminum craft that had been bobbing a slight distance away, came up beside the stranded Bayliner. After a few moments it moved ahead, and a tow line was plainly visible between them.

"Who's in the fishing boat?" Megan asked Tom, squinting to make out the figures.

"Some guy I've never seen before," he replied. "And I *think* it's your friend Gabby."

"Gabby?" Megan said in astonishment. "It can't be."

As the boats moved into the breakers, the boy guiding the fishing boat stood up and shouted. "Can somebody give us a hand?" Tom Hooper and several Leesville guys walked toward the water to bring them ashore. Megan joined them.

Gabrielle's face brightened into a big smile as she watched Megan rush knee-deep into the water.

"Gabby!" Megan greeted her happily as she grabbed the bow of the fishing boat. "You came!"

"It's a good thing I did, too. Brock left Alyssa stranded in the middle of the bay."

"Oh, no!" Megan took Gabrielle's hand and helped her step over the front of the boat into the shallow water.

Gabrielle turned and smiled at Bradley. "Thanks for the lift, Bradley."

He grinned and waved. "Anytime."

By then enough people had caught the Bayliner to keep it from drifting away, and Dylan untied the tow line. Bradley backed out beyond the breakers and sped off.

Megan turned to Gabrielle. "Bradley?"

"He's a nice boy who likes to fish," Gabrielle said matter-of-factly. "And that's it."

"Too bad." Megan gestured to Alyssa, who was still huddled in the other boat, and whispered, "How is she?"

Gabrielle glanced quickly over her shoulder. "Not too good. Luckily, Dylan's with her."

The two girls waded onto the beach, then turned and watched Dylan hop into the water and lift Alyssa out of the boat. He carried her in his arms and deposited her on the beach a little way from the crowd of onlookers.

Alyssa shook his hand and leaned forward as if to whisper something in his ear. Dylan smiled, then jogged back toward the water. An Ashton boy followed him with a red gas can and the two waded back out to the Bayliner.

"What did she say to Dylan?" Megan asked Gabrielle.

Gabrielle shrugged. "I guess she was thanking him."

"For what?" Shannon cut in, suddenly appearing beside them with Monica and the other cheerleaders. "For breaking up her relationship with Brock?"

"Shannon," Megan said impatiently, "Brock and Alyssa had problems *long* before she met Dylan."

"Oh, really? Look at her." Shannon pointed to Alyssa who stood alone. "She has guilt written all over her face."

Megan turned to Shannon. "Shannon, shut up!"

Shannon was so startled she stumbled sideways into Monica. "What did you say to me?"

"I said, shut up," Megan repeated carefully. "You are such a snob. You walk all over people with no regard for their feelings. I can't believe I ever considered you a friend. You don't know the meaning of the word."

For the first time in her life, the head cheerleader and self-appointed leader of the social set at Leesville High was absolutely speechless.

Alyssa walked away from the crowd of curious people. She reached the far side of the small island and stared out at the lights of Coconut Beach. In two short days her life had been turned inside out. She and Brock were through, that much was clear. She felt depressed and a little frightened at the thought of facing life without him. At the same time, it was as if the blackboard that was her life had been suddenly erased, and she was starting over with a clean slate.

Someone coughed behind her. Alyssa turned and saw Gabrielle.

"Alyssa," Gabrielle said softly. "Are you okay?"

Alyssa smiled and nodded. "I think so. I'm a little shaky, but other than that, I'm all right."

"Brock was awfully angry," Gabrielle said. "Maybe he'll cool down."

"I'm sure he will." Alyssa wrapped her arms around herself. "And maybe someday we'll be able to sit down and talk about all this rationally."

"Someday? So you think you guys are really finished?"

Alyssa took a deep breath. "I'll miss him. And maybe I'll always love him. He was my first boyfriend, after all. And he always meant well, but it had to end." Alyssa tilted her head back to look at the first few stars in the evening sky. "For the past few months I've felt as if I've had a time bomb ticking away inside me. And suddenly, it exploded."

"You want to see an explosion?" Megan came up beside the two girls. She gestured with her thumb over her shoulder. "You should see Shannon. She's so mad at me she can't see straight."

"What happened?" Alyssa asked.

Megan folded her arms across her chest. "I finally told her off and she didn't like it very much." Megan smiled sheepishly at Gabrielle. "Just like I didn't like it earlier this evening when you told me off."

Gabrielle blushed. "About that . . . I'm sorry I—"

"No," Megan cut in. "I'm sorry I—"

"But you didn't," Gabrielle insisted. "I'm the—"

"Oh, no," Megan insisted, putting her hands on her hips. "I'm the one who was pigheaded."

"What is this, some kind of code?" Alyssa asked.

Megan and Gabrielle answered in unison. "It's an apology."

The corners of Alyssa's mouth turned up in an amused smile. "As only you two could make one."

Gabrielle burst out laughing and Megan draped her arms around the two girls' shoulders. "What do you say we three bachelorettes have some fun?"

"I'm all for that," Alyssa said. "I think. No, I *know*. I'm going to put Brock behind me, and . . ."

Megan turned to see what Alyssa was looking at. A tall boy stood a little way up the beach, watching them. Megan finished Alyssa's sentence for her. "And put Dylan in front of you."

Alyssa looked at Gabrielle who added, "That would be my recommendation."

"Thanks, you guys!" Alyssa said.

"For what?" Megan asked.

"For being my friends. And, well . . ." Alyssa shrugged. "Just for being you." Her cheeks were flushed and her eyes sparkled as she looked toward Dylan. Gabrielle and Megan gave her a slight nudge and she ran off toward him.

"Do you really think it's our friendship that's cheered her up?" Megan asked as they watched Dylan and Alyssa disappear over a dune.

"Right." Gabrielle laughed.

"What say you and I take a stroll down by the bonfire? Maybe a boatful of hunks has just landed." She raised her eyebrows. "Who knows? Maybe your guy from the Paradise Café is with them."

"There you go again! Boys, boys, boys!" Gabrielle laughed and hugged Megan. "But you know what? I'm glad you're you, too!"

"Aren't you glad I invited you to Coconut Beach?" Megan asked as she looped her arm through Gabrielle's.

"Some invitation," Gabrielle retorted. "Crashing your car into my Mustang."

Megan's voice carried across the night air. "I didn't crash into you. You crashed into *me*."

Coming Attractions

Here's a preview of what's coming up
in Book #2 in the SPRING BREAK series:
Beach Boys.

Tentatively, Trevor brushed her lips with his. Gabrielle's pulse pounded like the surf. Wild thoughts clashed with trembling sensations as she responded to his kiss.

A first kiss had never been so romantic.

Afterward, still trying to catch her breath, she laid her head on Trevor's shoulder. His arm stayed firmly around her, and she wondered if he could feel the tremors just under her skin.

"It's strange," she said. "We've known each other such a short time, but I feel as if I've known you forever. You're different, Trevor. Not like all the other bums on the beach."

"What bums are those?" he asked, lifting the wisps of hair that had fallen from her French braid and placing a tiny row of kisses along her neck.

"Oh, you know. All those jerks on the beach who only have one thing in mind—and it isn't jogging."

"Water skiing?" Trevor laughed lightly.

"Not that, either. No, I'm talking about the guys who parade around half naked, showing off their tans and their muscles, thinking every bikini-clad female on the beach will swoon in their presence."

"You don't, huh?"

"Are you kidding?" Gabrielle whispered. She was having a great deal of difficulty continuing the conversation with Trevor blowing in her ear. She didn't really want to have a conversation, anyway. She wanted to be kissed again.

But Trevor persisted. "You mean, you're not turned on by the meat parade?"

"No," she said. "But one of my roommates is. From the minute we broke down on the road and had to catch a lift with two frat guys, Megan's done nothing but go after guys. Now she's hung up on that lifeguard who holds court in front of the Cabana Banana."

Trevor coughed. "Lifeguard?"

"I'm sure you've seen him," Gabrielle scoffed. "At least, you must have seen his harem. The girls swarm around him like bees. It's so vulgar and so stupid. There's *no way* I'd fall for a guy like that!"

Trevor stiffened and took his arm from Gabrielle's shoulder. "Well, uh, I hate to cut this conversation short, but I think we'd better be getting back."

Before Gabrielle had a chance to question his sudden change in mood, he stood up and started walking toward the path. The colorful birds scattered before him.

Gabrielle stared at his retreating back.

When she didn't follow immediately, he retraced his steps, grabbed her hand, and hauled her to her feet.

"Trevor, is something wrong?" Gabrielle asked worriedly.

"Nope. It's just getting late, that's all. You never know when a tropical storm could come up and surprise you. My boat is too small to handle much chop."

"Oh. Of course."

They emerged onto the beach a few minutes later. Trevor seemed like a completely different person from the one he had been only a few minutes before. Then, he had been kissing her neck. Now, he was revving up the motor and making a beeline for the pier.

Gabrielle couldn't enjoy the lovely sight of the Coconut Beach shoreline. She was too con-

cerned with trying to figure out what had upset
Trevor. He didn't seem mad, exactly. Just dis-
tant.

When they reached the pier, Gabrielle made
one last attempt to capture the feeling they had
shared on the island only a short while before.

"I really want to thank you again for a great
afternoon," she said, moving close to him.

"I had a nice time, too," Trevor answered distractedly. He bent his head and kissed her
briefly. "I hope I can see you again some time."
He waved and walked off.

Gabrielle stood and watched him go.

What had happened to her perfect afternoon?